Vampires in Literature

BOOK ONE

A FOREWORD TO THE COLLECTION

Compiled by Michael Toeset, Robert Kimbrell
Forward by Robert Kimbrell

Edition One: 2025

ISBN Paperback: 978-1-950464-71-5
ISBN eBook: 978-1-950464-73-9

Other books and publisher information:
ReadAdventures.com

Vampires in Literature

BOOK ONE

A FOREWORD TO THE COLLECTION

Compiled by

Michael Toeset

&

Robert Kimbrell

CONTENTS

Collection
Foreword

Those only familiar with the subject of vampires as it pertains to the ebb and flows of pop culture will be aware of modern books and films, and will know about (but likely not have read) the classic Dracula, by Bram Stoker. This may approximate the extent of their knowledge.

Passing over the many types in between, we find on the contrasting end those deeply familiar with the vampire subject. (Cultists are not here, and they are not a subsection. At best, cultists are in parallel, but are unrelated.) Those on this end are aware of the vastness of vampirism throughout history. They are on some level students, enthralled fans of the subject. We created this book collection for anyone along the spectrum with an interest.

Most undertakings cannot possibly encompass all knowledge of any wide-ranging subject. The same is true of blood-consuming, undead vampire folklore. In the interest of setting up this collection properly, we will skim the outer rims enough to set the stage for our collection theme. Vampirism is arguably the most romanticized genre in literature. We love to read the stories and imagine life with a vampire or even as a vampire. In preparing for this collection, we dug deep, and parsed all the accurate information we could find. It will be deflating to some, but we could find no real evidence of vampirism anywhere, anytime throughout history. Would it really be good to have undead among us, hunting for satiating hemoglobin?

Someone may say, "But there have been

Etymology of the English word vampire is somewhat unclear. Both the French and Germans used vampyre and vampir, respectively. Some claim a Lithuanian origin, some Serbian. A vampiric term Upyri comes from old Russian (11-13th century).

those in history that consumed blood" or "What about Renfield's Syndrome?"

Fair point. Let's address this a bit more scientifically. According to academic sources and papers(a), there are a small number of people who may exhibit behavioral manifestations such as blood-drinking. Again, this is a behavioral manifestation of a very real diagnosis, such as schizophrenia. One can even fetishize blood-drinking, but fetishizing is not a syndrome and does not a vampire make. There is also a blood disorder called porphyria. Those who suffer from this disorder may have many symptoms including a sunlight oversensitivity, but this doesn't make them a vampire.

For our discussion here and within this collection, when we say "vampire" we refer to the actual mythical, undead creature (a being, usually human) who thirsts for blood. The craving for blood is not imagined or created, but rather part of the essence of the being. We're also not talking about so-called financial vampires or psychic vampires, or any other variation.

(a) Oppawasky. (n.d.). Vampirism: clinical vampirism--Renfield's syndrome.(CE ARTICLE: 1 CE CREDIT: A CASE STUDY)(Cover story)(Case study). *Annals of the American Psychotherapy Association.*, *13*(4), 58–63. https://doi.org/info:doi/

Destruction of a vampire skeleton; from a
French book, sometime around 1900

Real Bloody Times

This all doesn't mean history is without its intriguing moments of bloody gore and violence, and these are worth a mention to set the stage for the fiction which follows. For instance, there have been dozens of documented cases of vampire rituals in New England that began in the 1700s. (So-called healers from Europe and ignorance about tuberculosis contributed to these "undead" experiences.) Look into vampires and the undead. Search results will keep you busy for hours. Accounts and versions of events available to us today are difficult if not impossible to verify. There are usually elements of truth in many of these, but when it comes to what we know to be true from comparing it with reality, we see the irrational. Often we can reasonably conclude what likely didn't happen based on historical context as well.

Though they are not vampire stories per se, some very real and bloody stories have stood the tests of time. Could it be that our desire for vampirism to be true is such that we wish to associate these with authentic vampirism? It oftentimes seems to be the case. Two deserving characters in history tease our inner blood-sucker. You have likely heard of them. These stories fill a void within us that is both curious and hungry for the dark and fantastic—even if the reality is horrific.

Painting of Elizabeth Bathory at 25 years of age, a copy of a now lost original portrait from 1585; likely painted in the 16th century; by an anonymous artist. (Public domain, via Wikimedia Commons)

Elizabeth Bathory, a noblewoman of Hungary (1650-1614), tortured and killed hundreds of women and girls. Some sources claim accusations against her were fabricated for political reasons, and there may be some element of truth to this. Even amidst the blurs of history the facts remain: Elizabeth Bathory was a killer who tortured many.

Vlad Tepes (Romanian), also known as Vlad III and Vlad the Impaler (1431-1476), is probably the most famous and recognizable figure. While Prince of Wallachia, his efforts to defend Christian Europe against the Ottoman attacks were, and still are, spine-chilling. His acts terrified the Ottomans, and images such as the one included below, spur us to imagine the bloody horrific scene.

Vlad III; a hand-colored woodcut from 1488; artist unknown.

Vlad enjoys his meal near a forest of his
impaled victims.

Beyond Elizabeth Bathory and Vlad Tepes, we can delve further into more obscure stories such as that of Serbian peasant Peter Plogojowitz, who was believed to have risen from the dead. We can find the story of Jure Grando, who according to records, may be the first person ever described as a "vampire."

(Also see *"Berwick-Upon-Tweed"* in back of book for one of the earliest noteworthy accounts in Britain.)

Though we can value and relish these stories, there really is no indisputable evidence that these bloody realities were true vampires in the undead sense of the word. We do not wish to diminish any truth within these stories. Much research has in fact been done into these. Yet, how can we be confident these accounts equal concrete evidence? As distasteful as it may be to sound like a skeptic, we prefer to err on the side of reason when it comes to considering what may be true. For example, there may indeed be eyewitnesses to the aforementioned Jure Grando events. On the other hand, it may also be true that in writing of Jure Grando, Johann Joseph von Goerre (a German historian and journalist), took liberties, enhancing the story. We think it is also vital to remember that this story, like so many others, took place before the Age of Enlightenment (aka The Age of Reason)(b).

BECAUSE REALITY IS ALL AROUND US, FOR OUR VERY SANITY we must enjoy our fantasies. We can explore and build upon our fantasies in the fiction available to us. Fiction is our secret experience, our private indulgence in which to escape. Our spark of curiosity builds, and we make a concerted effort to quench thirst with the vampire-related.

Folklore may provide real sustenance. There is another tale, the tale of Croglin Grange. We mention the Irish Dearg Due, the Baobhan Sith, the Scottish Succubus with her sexy hooves. We mention the Manananggal of the Philippines with its fangs and wings. There is the flying snake in Chile who can shape shift, called Peuchen.

More research leads to more digging. Whether described as vampires or other variation, we uncover more mythical figures and blood-drinkers such as Lilith, Lilitu, goddess Kali from ancient India, Egyptian goddess Sekhmet. Greek mythology provides a truly awesome story about Lamia. There is much more we could discuss here, but doing so moves us beyond the scope of this book and collection. We encourage you to become an explorer.

*In back of book, also see comments from ***Voltaire's Philosophical Dictionary*** regarding vampires.

Duignan, Brian. "Enlightenment". *Encyclopedia Britannica*, 15 Sep. 2024, https://www.britannica.com/event/Enlightenment-European-history. Accessed 25 October 2024.

Cultural Mentions

Out of our own appreciation for early twentieth-century nostalgia, we lend a cursory glance. Because we exist in the present age, or time, we tend to have a narrow scope of view, as if something is particular only to our time. But we cannot forget that vampires (or vampirism) have been around for centuries, and have on some level permeated cultures around the world. Western culture in particular has had its fun as it relates to entertainment.

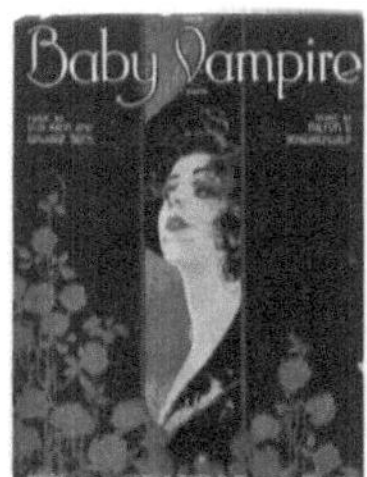

Three examples of sheet music. Left: Sheet music for the song Baby Vampire in flapper era, c1917; Middle: a waltz c1911; Right: sheet music for the infamous Ziegfeld Follies, published 1914.

The theme of vampires was hijacked in political cartoons by some, including the well-known Herbert Block (Herblock). In one cartoon, he depicts a large "capitalist" vampire bat swooping down on the U.S. capital. (Image unavailable.) The premise is of course absurd, as if an alternative system which reduces citizens to serfs and removes their freedom to trade is better. The way people choose to exploit cultural phenomenon are telling.

Cartoon from 1898, by Norman Jennet. At the bottom it says, "The Vampire that hovers over North Carolina"-Promoting the disgraceful idea that black people in political power are a danger to white people.(c)

Norman Ethre Jennett, "The Vampire that Hovers Over North Carolina," News and Observer, September 27, 1898, The North Carolina Election of 1898, North Carolina Collection, University of North Carolina at Chapel Hill, http://www.lib.unc.edu/ncc/1898/sources/cartoons/0927.html (accessed November 10, 2024).

Comic on left from 1972; right from 1953

Comic books with a vampire theme have remained popular through the years. The first comic book to feature a vampire? *Batman versus the Vampire* was a two-parter that appeared in **Detective Comics** in 1939. It is easy to stop there, but further digging reveals a lesser-known and handsome character (created by New Fun Comics, now DC Comics) named Dr. Occult. Issue #6, *The Vampire Master*, was published in 1935.

Dr. Occult

It was natural for vampires to creep into theatres. This one a Fulton theatre playbill from 1928.

Dorothy Peterson played the role of Lucy
Seward in 1924 theatre production of Dracula.
She would go on to act in over 80 films.

Palace Theatre in Sydney Australia, 1929.

Countless films have been made, many of which we could perhaps consider somewhat cheesy in comparison to styles and methods of today. They deserve respect, however, for bringing unique fears into the soul of culture at the time. Those films which mark the *beginning* of the exploration of vampirism deserve utmost reverence. *Nosferatu* (1922) is considered the first vampire film. The film was directed by F.W. Murnau, an influential filmmaker of the silent era. Count Orlock was played by actor Max Schreck.

A still from the film Nosferatu; actor Max Schreck plays Count Orlock.

We are aware of Christopher Lee, who played Dracula in 1958 in *Horror of Dracula*. Who has not heard the name of his Dracula predecessor, Bela Lugosi?

Movie poster from the 1970 film, Count Dracula; starring Christopher Lee.

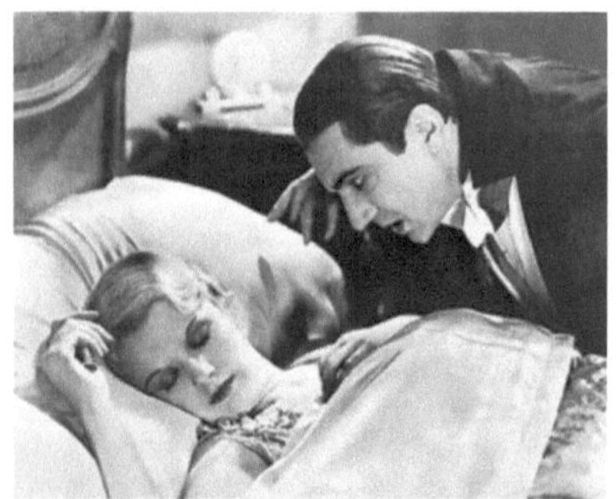

In Dracula (1931), Bela Lugosi considers the neck of actress Francis Dade.

We repeat: None of this is intended to be a complete listing of all vampire comic books, plays, films, etc. In fact, in compiling this information, it was difficult to stop diving headfirst to include every tidbit of information. So this foreword will serve to merely whet our appetites for the fangtastic reads which follow.

Onward Toward Literary Fiction

Regarding the poetry which follows in this fore-word edition. As previously stated, our focus is the topic of vampires, in the mythical and undead sense of the word. We found a number of poems, however, which are noteworthy or even masterful, but do not truly fit into the vampire subgenre. Still, because space allows, we did opt to include these for your enjoyment. For instance, Rudyard Kipling's "The Vampire" is about a heartless woman and a foolish man in love with her.

In book 2 of this collection, we have a plethora of short stories, and we made it as comprehensive as possible. For example, were you aware that there is another vampire tale from Bram Stoker that was published by his widow posthumously? You have likely heard of "Carmilla", but have you heard of Clarimonde? "The Dead Woman in Love" (La Morte amoureuse; French), is about a woman named Clarimonde who is a vampire, and the priest who fell for her. Of course, we include "The Vampyre", by John William Polidori. Published in 1819, "The Black Vampire; a Legend of St. Domingo", is about a black slave who rose as a vampire after being buried. The very long "Varney the Vampire" (published in penny dreadfuls starting in 1845), and British author Florence Marryat's "The Blood of the Vampire" are also happily included. There will be more beyond those mentioned here. When possible, images will be included, with special consideration given to original images when available.

When it comes to these short stories, it is not enough for it to mention a vampire or for the title to contain the word "Vampire". For all the prose in this collection, our focus is writings with honest blood-sucking vampirism as a subject. For example, bibliophiles or Sherlock Holmes fans may be familiar with "The Adventure of the Sussex Vampire", by Arthur Conan Doyle. This story is a worthy classic, but the mystery does not actually include a vampire, it only appears that way. The suspicion of a vampire culprit is merely a vehicle which drives the mystery.

It is our sincere hope that all the books in this collection round out your library and offer you many hours of reading enjoyment. So we begin...

But first, on earth as vampire sent,
Thy corse shall from its tomb be rent:
Then ghastly haunt thy native place,
And suck the blood of all thy race.

From Giaour,
by Lord Byron

At this time the publisher wishes to kindly broach three issues.

First, our priority in every case is to present every work accurately, as it was originally published or presented. No grammatical or spelling changes were made to any of the texts in this collection.

However, on rare occasions, an obvious punctuational error was present due to human error in translation or transliteration. Also, in some instances, punctuation was present in the source text that could not have existed in the original text itself. In these cases, we corrected or removed only the punctuation, and retained the meaning intended by the author. You may still notice odd punctuation, such as a colon followed by two dashes. These are either present in the original early work, or added over time. These may not make for a pretty reading page, but these are retained because we could not reasonably determine when they were added.

Second, it is possible that some texts or parts of texts may be offensive in subject or language. We assume the reader to be mature and discerning, therefore realizing that often such writings as presented here are from a different time and/or within a different context.

Lastly, much of the poetry ahead has at some point been translated into English. When translator information is available to us, we make it known, as is proper to do.

Thank you.

Poetry

The Vampire
Rudyard Kipling

A fool there was and he made his prayer
(Even as you or I!)
To a rag and a bone and a hank of hair,
(We called her the woman who did not care),
But the fool he called her his lady fair—
(Even as you or I!)
Oh, the years we waste and the tears we waste,
And the work of our head and hand
Belong to the woman who did not know
(And now we know that she never could know)
And did not understand!

A fool there was and his goods he spent,
(Even as you or I!)
Honour and faith and a sure intent
(And it wasn't the least what the lady meant),
But a fool must follow his natural bent
(Even as you or I!)

Oh, the toil we lost and the spoil we lost
And the excellent things we planned
Belong to the woman who didn't know why
(And now we know that she never knew why)
And did not understand!

The fool was stripped to his foolish hide,
(Even as you or I!)
Which she might have seen when she threw him aside—
(But it isn't on record the lady tried)
So some of him lived but the most of him died—
(Even as you or I!)

And it isn't the shame and it isn't the blame
That stings like a white-hot brand—
It's coming to know that she never knew why
(Seeing, at last, she could never know why)
And never could understand!

Painting by Philip Burne-Jones, *The Vampire* (1897) which inspired the above Kipling poem.

The Vampyre
John Stagg

(No image available)
"Why looks my lord so deadly pale?
Why fades the crimson from his cheek?
What can my dearest husband ail?
Thy heartfelt cares, O Herman, speak!

"Why, at the silent hour of rest,
Dost thou in sleep so sadly mourn?
Has tho' with heaviest grief oppress'd,
Griefs too distressful to be borne.

"Why heaves thy breast? — why throbs thy heart?
O speak! and if there be relief
Thy Gertrude solace shall impart,
If not, at least shall share thy grief.

"Wan is that cheek, which once the bloom
Of manly beauty sparkling shew'd;

Dim are those eyes, in pensive gloom,
That late with keenest lustre glow'd.
"Say why, too, at the midnight hour,
You sadly pant and tug for breath,
As if some supernat'ral pow'r
Were pulling you away to death?

"Restless, tho' sleeping, still you groan,
And with convulsive horror start;
O Herman! to thy wife make known
That grief which preys upon thy heart."

"O Gertrude! how shall I relate
Th' uncommon anguish that I feel;
Strange as severe is this my fate, —
A fate I cannot long conceal.

"In spite of all my wonted strength,
Stern destiny has seal'd my doom;
The dreadful malady at length
Wil drag me to the silent tomb!"

"But say, my Herman, what's the cause
Of this distress, and all thy care.
That, vulture-like, thy vitals gnaws,
And galls thy bosom with despair?

"Sure this can be no common grief,
Sure this can be no common pain?
Speak, if this world contain relief,
That soon thy Gertrude shall obtain."

"O Gertrude, 'tis a horrid cause,
O Gertrude, 'tis unusual care,
That, vulture-like, my vitals gnaws,
And galls my bosom with despair.

"Young Sigismund, my once dear friend,
But lately he resign'd his breath;
With others I did him attend
Unto the silent house of death.

"For him I wept, for him I mourn'd,
Paid all to friendship that was due;
But sadly friendship is return'd,
Thy Herman he must follow too!

"Must follow to the gloomy grave,
In spite of human art or skill;
No pow'r on earth my life can save,
'Tis fate's unalterable will!

"Young Sigismund, my once dear friend,
But now my persecutor foul,
Doth his malevolence extend
E'en to the torture of my soul.

"By night, when, wrapt in soundest sleep,
All mortals share a soft repose,
My soul doth dreadful vigils keep,
More keen than which hell scarely knows.

VAMPIRES IN LITERATURE

"From the drear mansion of the tomb,
From the low regions of the dead,
The ghost of Sigismund doth roam,
And dreadful haunts me in my bed!

"There, vested in infernal guise,
(By means to me not understood,)
Close to my side the goblin lies,
And drinks away my vital blood!

"Sucks from my veins the streaming life,
And drains the fountain of my heart!
O Gertrude, Gertrude! dearest wife!
Unutterable is my smart.

"When surfeited, the goblin dire,
With banqueting by suckled gore,
Will to his sepulchre retire,
Till night invites him forth once more.

"Then will he dreadfully return,
And from my veins life's juices drain;
Whilst, slumb'ring, I with anguish mourn,
And toss with agonizing pain!

"Already I'm exhausted, spent;
His carnival is nearly o'er,
My soul with agony is rent,
To-morrow I shall be no more!

"But, O my Gertrude! dearest wife!

The keenest pangs hath last remain'd—
When dead, I too shall seek thy life,
Thy blood by Herman shall be drain'd!

"But to avoid this horrid fate,
Soon as I'm dead and laid in earth,
Drive thro' my corpse a jav'lin straight; —
This shall prevent my coming forth.

"O watch with me, this last sad night,
Watch in your chamber here alone,
But carefully conceal the light
Until you hear my parting groan.

"Then at what time the vesper-bell
Of yonder convent shall be toll'd,
That peal shall ring my passing knell,
And Herman's body shall be cold!

"Then, and just then, thy lamp make bare,
The starting ray, the bursting light,
Shall from my side the goblin scare,
And shew him visible to sight!"

The live-long night poor Gertrude sate,
Watch'd by her sleeping, dying lord;
The live-long night she mourn'd his fate,
The object whom her soul ador'd.

Then at what time the vesper-bell
Of yonder convent sadly toll'd,

The, then was peal'd his passing knell,
The hapless Herman he was cold!
Just at that moment Gertrude drew
From 'neath her cloak the hidden light;
When, dreadful! she beheld in view
The shade of Sigismund! — sad sight!

Indignant roll'd his ireful eyes,
That gleam'd with wild horrific stare;
And fix'd a moment with surprise,
Beheld aghast th' enlight'ning glare.

His jaws cadaverous were besmear'd
With clott'd carnage o'er and o'er,
And all his horrid whole appear'd
Distent, and fill'd with human gore!

With hideous scowl the spectre fled;
She shriek'd aloud; — then swoon'd away!
The hapless Herman in his bed,
All pale, a lifeless body lay!

Next day in council 'twas decree,
(Urg'd at the instance of the state,)
That shudd'ring nature should be freed
From pests like these ere 'twas too late.

The choir then burst the fun'ral dome
Where Sigismund was lately laid,
And found him, tho' within the tomb,
Still warm as life, and undecay'd.

With blood his visage was distain'd,
Ensanguin'd were his frightful eyes,
Each sign of former life remain'd,
Save that all motionless he lies.

The corpse of Herman they contrive
To the same sepulchre to take,
And thro' both carcases they drive,
Deep in the earth, a sharpen'd stake!

By this was finish'd their career,
Thro' this no longer they can roam;
From them their friends have nought to fear,
Both quiet keep the slumb'ring tomb.

The Vampire
Madison Julius Cawein

VAMPIRES IN LITERATURE

A lily in a twilight place?
A moonflow'r in the lonely night?—
Strange beauty of a woman's face
Of wildflow'r-white!
The rain that hangs a star's green ray
Slim on a leaf-point's restlessness,
Is not so glimmering green and gray
As was her dress.

I drew her dark hair from her eyes,
And in their deeps beheld a while
Such shadowy moonlight as the skies
Of Hell may smile.

She held her mouth up redly wan,
And burning cold,—I bent and kissed
Such rosy snow as some wild dawn
Makes of a mist.

God shall not take from me that hour,
When round my neck her white arms clung!
When 'neath my lips, like some fierce flower,
Her white throat swung!

Or words she murmured while she leaned!
Witch-words, she holds me softly by,—
The spell that binds me to a fiend
Until I die.

Lamia

John Keats

Part 1

Upon a time, before the faery broods
Drove Nymph and Satyr from the prosperous woods,
Before King Oberon's bright diadem,
Sceptre, and mantle, clasp'd with dewy gem,
Frighted away the Dryads and the Fauns
From rushes green, and brakes, and cowslip'd lawns,
The ever-smitten Hermes empty left
His golden throne, bent warm on amorous theft:
From high Olympus had he stolen light,
On this side of Jove's clouds, to escape the sight
Of his great summoner, and made retreat
Into a forest on the shores of Crete.
For somewhere in that sacred island dwelt
A nymph, to whom all hoofed Satyrs knelt;
At whose white feet the languid Tritons poured
Pearls, while on land they wither'd and adored.
Fast by the springs where she to bathe was wont,
And in those meads where sometime she might haunt,
Were strewn rich gifts, unknown to any Muse,
Though Fancy's casket were unlock'd to choose.

Ah, what a world of love was at her feet!
So Hermes thought, and a celestial heat
Burnt from his winged heels to either ear,
That from a whiteness, as the lily clear,
Blush'd into roses 'mid his golden hair,
Fallen in jealous curls about his shoulders bare.
From vale to vale, from wood to wood, he flew,
Breathing upon the flowers his passion new,
And wound with many a river to its head,
To find where this sweet nymph prepar'd her secret bed:
In vain; the sweet nymph might nowhere be found,
And so he rested, on the lonely ground,
Pensive, and full of painful jealousies
Of the Wood-Gods, and even the very trees.
There as he stood, he heard a mournful voice,
Such as once heard, in gentle heart, destroys
All pain but pity: thus the lone voice spake:
"When from this wreathed tomb shall I awake!
When move in a sweet body fit for life,
And love, and pleasure, and the ruddy strife
Of hearts and lips! Ah, miserable me!"
The God, dove-footed, glided silently
Round bush and tree, soft-brushing, in his speed,
The taller grasses and full-flowering weed,
Until he found a palpitating snake,
Bright, and cirque-couchant in a dusky brake.

She was a gordian shape of dazzling hue,
Vermilion-spotted, golden, green, and blue;
Striped like a zebra, freckled like a pard,
Eyed like a peacock, and all crimson barr'd;
And full of silver moons, that, as she breathed,
Dissolv'd, or brighter shone, or interwreathed
Their lustres with the gloomier tapestries—
So rainbow-sided, touch'd with miseries,
She seem'd, at once, some penanced lady elf,
Some demon's mistress, or the demon's self.
Upon her crest she wore a wannish fire
Sprinkled with stars, like Ariadne's tiar:
Her head was serpent, but ah, bitter-sweet!
She had a woman's mouth with all its pearls complete:
And for her eyes: what could such eyes do there
But weep, and weep, that they were born so fair?
As Proserpine still weeps for her Sicilian air.
Her throat was serpent, but the words she spake
Came, as through bubbling honey, for Love's sake,
And thus; while Hermes on his pinions lay,
Like a stoop'd falcon ere he takes his prey.

"Fair Hermes, crown'd with feathers, fluttering light,
I had a splendid dream of thee last night:
I saw thee sitting, on a throne of gold,
Among the Gods, upon Olympus old,
The only sad one; for thou didst not hear
The soft, lute-finger'd Muses chaunting clear,
Nor even Apollo when he sang alone,
Deaf to his throbbing throat's long, long melodious moan.
I dreamt I saw thee, robed in purple flakes,
Break amorous through the clouds, as morning breaks,
And, swiftly as a bright Phoebean dart,
Strike for the Cretan isle; and here thou art!
Too gentle Hermes, hast thou found the maid?"
Whereat the star of Lethe not delay'd
His rosy eloquence, and thus inquired:
"Thou smooth-lipp'd serpent, surely high inspired!
Thou beauteous wreath, with melancholy eyes,
Possess whatever bliss thou canst devise,
Telling me only where my nymph is fled,—
Where she doth breathe!" "Bright planet, thou hast said,"
Return'd the snake, "but seal with oaths, fair God!"
"I swear," said Hermes, "by my serpent rod,
And by thine eyes, and by thy starry crown!"

Light flew his earnest words, among the blossoms blown.
Then thus again the brilliance feminine:
"Too frail of heart! for this lost nymph of thine,
Free as the air, invisibly, she strays
About these thornless wilds; her pleasant days
She tastes unseen; unseen her nimble feet
Leave traces in the grass and flowers sweet;
From weary tendrils, and bow'd branches green,
She plucks the fruit unseen, she bathes unseen:
And by my power is her beauty veil'd
To keep it unaffronted, unassail'd
By the love-glances of unlovely eyes,
Of Satyrs, Fauns, and blear'd Silenus' sighs.
Pale grew her immortality, for woe
Of all these lovers, and she grieved so
I took compassion on her, bade her steep
Her hair in weird syrops, that would keep
Her loveliness invisible, yet free
To wander as she loves, in liberty.
Thou shalt behold her, Hermes, thou alone,
If thou wilt, as thou swearest, grant my boon!"
Then, once again, the charmed God began
An oath, and through the serpent's ears it ran
Warm, tremulous, devout, psalterian.
Ravish'd, she lifted her Circean head,
Blush'd a live damask, and swift-lisping said,
"I was a woman, let me have once more
A woman's shape, and charming as before.

I love a youth of Corinth—O the bliss!
Give me my woman's form, and place me where he is.
Stoop, Hermes, let me breathe upon thy brow,
And thou shalt see thy sweet nymph even now."
The God on half-shut feathers sank serene,
She breath'd upon his eyes, and swift was seen
Of both the guarded nymph near-smiling on the green.
It was no dream; or say a dream it was,
Real are the dreams of Gods, and smoothly pass
Their pleasures in a long immortal dream.
One warm, flush'd moment, hovering, it might seem
Dash'd by the wood-nymph's beauty, so he burn'd;
Then, lighting on the printless verdure, turn'd
To the swoon'd serpent, and with languid arm,
Delicate, put to proof the lythe Caducean charm.
So done, upon the nymph his eyes he bent,
Full of adoring tears and blandishment,
And towards her stept: she, like a moon in wane,
Faded before him, cower'd, nor could restrain
Her fearful sobs, self-folding like a flower
That faints into itself at evening hour:
But the God fostering her chilled hand,
She felt the warmth, her eyelids open'd bland,
And, like new flowers at morning song of bees,
Bloom'd, and gave up her honey to the lees.
Into the green-recessed woods they flew;
Nor grew they pale, as mortal lovers do.

Left to herself, the serpent now began
To change; her elfin blood in madness ran,
Her mouth foam'd, and the grass, therewith besprent,
Wither'd at dew so sweet and virulent;
Her eyes in torture fix'd, and anguish drear,
Hot, glaz'd, and wide, with lid-lashes all sear,
Flash'd phosphor and sharp sparks, without one cool-
ing tear.
The colours all inflam'd throughout her train,
She writh'd about, convuls'd with scarlet pain:
A deep volcanian yellow took the place
Of all her milder-mooned body's grace;
And, as the lava ravishes the mead,
Spoilt all her silver mail, and golden brede;
Made gloom of all her frecklings, streaks and bars,
Eclips'd her crescents, and lick'd up her stars:
So that, in moments few, she was undrest
Of all her sapphires, greens, and amethyst,
And rubious-argent: of all these bereft,
Nothing but pain and ugliness were left.
Still shone her crown; that vanish'd, also she
Melted and disappear'd as suddenly;
And in the air, her new voice luting soft,
Cried, "Lycius! gentle Lycius!"—Borne aloft
With the bright mists about the mountains hoar
These words dissolv'd: Crete's forests heard no more.

Whither fled Lamia, now a lady bright,
A full-born beauty new and exquisite?
She fled into that valley they pass o'er
Who go to Corinth from Cenchreas' shore;
And rested at the foot of those wild hills,
The rugged founts of the Peraean rills,
And of that other ridge whose barren back
Stretches, with all its mist and cloudy rack,
South-westward to Cleone. There she stood
About a young bird's flutter from a wood,
Fair, on a sloping green of mossy tread,
By a clear pool, wherein she passioned
To see herself escap'd from so sore ills,
While her robes flaunted with the daffodils.

Ah, happy Lycius!—for she was a maid
More beautiful than ever twisted braid,
Or sigh'd, or blush'd, or on spring-flowered lea
Spread a green kirtle to the minstrelsy:
A virgin purest lipp'd, yet in the lore
Of love deep learned to the red heart's core:
Not one hour old, yet of sciential brain
To unperplex bliss from its neighbour pain;
Define their pettish limits, and estrange
Their points of contact, and swift counterchange;
Intrigue with the specious chaos, and dispart
Its most ambiguous atoms with sure art;
As though in Cupid's college she had spent
Sweet days a lovely graduate, still unshent,
And kept his rosy terms in idle languishment.

Why this fair creature chose so fairily
By the wayside to linger, we shall see;
But first 'tis fit to tell how she could muse
And dream, when in the serpent prison-house,
Of all she list, strange or magnificent:
How, ever, where she will'd, her spirit went;
Whether to faint Elysium, or where
Down through tress-lifting waves the Nereids fair
Wind into Thetis' bower by many a pearly stair;
Or where God Bacchus drains his cups divine,
Stretch'd out, at ease, beneath a glutinous pine;
Or where in Pluto's gardens palatine
Mulciber's columns gleam in far piazzian line.
And sometimes into cities she would send
Her dream, with feast and rioting to blend;
And once, while among mortals dreaming thus,
She saw the young Corinthian Lycius
Charioting foremost in the envious race,
Like a young Jove with calm uneager face,
And fell into a swooning love of him.
Now on the moth-time of that evening dim
He would return that way, as well she knew,
To Corinth from the shore; for freshly blew
The eastern soft wind, and his galley now
Grated the quaystones with her brazen prow
In port Cenchreas, from Egina isle
Fresh anchor'd; whither he had been awhile
To sacrifice to Jove, whose temple there
Waits with high marble doors for blood and incense rare.

Jove heard his vows, and better'd his desire;
For by some freakful chance he made retire
From his companions, and set forth to walk,
Perhaps grown wearied of their Corinth talk:
Over the solitary hills he fared,
Thoughtless at first, but ere eve's star appeared
His phantasy was lost, where reason fades,
In the calm'd twilight of Platonic shades.
Lamia beheld him coming, near, more near—
Close to her passing, in indifference drear,
His silent sandals swept the mossy green;
So neighbour'd to him, and yet so unseen
She stood: he pass'd, shut up in mysteries,
His mind wrapp'd like his mantle, while her eyes
Follow'd his steps, and her neck regal white
Turn'd—syllabling thus, "Ah, Lycius bright,
And will you leave me on the hills alone?
Lycius, look back! and be some pity shown."
He did; not with cold wonder fearingly,
But Orpheus-like at an Eurydice;
For so delicious were the words she sung,
It seem'd he had lov'd them a whole summer long:
And soon his eyes had drunk her beauty up,
Leaving no drop in the bewildering cup,
And still the cup was full,—while he afraid
Lest she should vanish ere his lip had paid
Due adoration, thus began to adore;
Her soft look growing coy, she saw his chain so sure:
"Leave thee alone! Look back! Ah, Goddess, see
Whether my eyes can ever turn from thee!
For pity do not this sad heart belie—
Even as thou vanishest so I shall die.

Stay! though a Naiad of the rivers, stay!
To thy far wishes will thy streams obey:
Stay! though the greenest woods be thy domain,
Alone they can drink up the morning rain:
Though a descended Pleiad, will not one
Of thine harmonious sisters keep in tune
Thy spheres, and as thy silver proxy shine?
So sweetly to these ravish'd ears of mine
Came thy sweet greeting, that if thou shouldst fade
Thy memory will waste me to a shade—
For pity do not melt!"—"If I should stay,"
Said Lamia, "here, upon this floor of clay,
And pain my steps upon these flowers too rough,
What canst thou say or do of charm enough
To dull the nice remembrance of my home?
Thou canst not ask me with thee here to roam
Over these hills and vales, where no joy is,—
Empty of immortality and bliss!
Thou art a scholar, Lycius, and must know
That finer spirits cannot breathe below
In human climes, and live: Alas! poor youth,
What taste of purer air hast thou to soothe
My essence? What serener palaces,
Where I may all my many senses please,
And by mysterious sleights a hundred thirsts appease?
It cannot be—Adieu!" So said, she rose
Tiptoe with white arms spread. He, sick to lose
The amorous promise of her lone complain,
Swoon'd, murmuring of love, and pale with pain.

The cruel lady, without any show
Of sorrow for her tender favourite's woe,
But rather, if her eyes could brighter be,
With brighter eyes and slow amenity,
Put her new lips to his, and gave afresh
The life she had so tangled in her mesh:
And as he from one trance was wakening
Into another, she began to sing,
Happy in beauty, life, and love, and every thing,
A song of love, too sweet for earthly lyres,
While, like held breath, the stars drew in their panting fires
And then she whisper'd in such trembling tone,
As those who, safe together met alone
For the first time through many anguish'd days,
Use other speech than looks; bidding him raise
His drooping head, and clear his soul of doubt,
For that she was a woman, and without
Any more subtle fluid in her veins
Than throbbing blood, and that the self-same pains
Inhabited her frail-strung heart as his.

And next she wonder'd how his eyes could miss
Her face so long in Corinth, where, she said,
She dwelt but half retir'd, and there had led
Days happy as the gold coin could invent
Without the aid of love; yet in content
Till she saw him, as once she pass'd him by,
Where 'gainst a column he leant thoughtfully
At Venus' temple porch, 'mid baskets heap'd
Of amorous herbs and flowers, newly reap'd
Late on that eve, as 'twas the night before
The Adonian feast; whereof she saw no more,
But wept alone those days, for why should she adore?
Lycius from death awoke into amaze,
To see her still, and singing so sweet lays;
Then from amaze into delight he fell
To hear her whisper woman's lore so well;
And every word she spake entic'd him on
To unperplex'd delight and pleasure known.
Let the mad poets say whate'er they please
Of the sweets of Fairies, Peris, Goddesses,
There is not such a treat among them all,
Haunters of cavern, lake, and waterfall,
As a real woman, lineal indeed
From Pyrrha's pebbles or old Adam's seed.
Thus gentle Lamia judg'd, and judg'd aright,
That Lycius could not love in half a fright,
So threw the goddess off, and won his heart
More pleasantly by playing woman's part,
With no more awe than what her beauty gave,
That, while it smote, still guaranteed to save.

Lycius to all made eloquent reply,
Marrying to every word a twinborn sigh;
And last, pointing to Corinth, ask'd her sweet,
If 'twas too far that night for her soft feet.
The way was short, for Lamia's eagerness
Made, by a spell, the triple league decrease
To a few paces; not at all surmised
By blinded Lycius, so in her comprized.
They pass'd the city gates, he knew not how
So noiseless, and he never thought to know.

As men talk in a dream, so Corinth all,
Throughout her palaces imperial,
And all her populous streets and temples lewd,
Mutter'd, like tempest in the distance brew'd,
To the wide-spreaded night above her towers.
Men, women, rich and poor, in the cool hours,
Shuffled their sandals o'er the pavement white,
Companion'd or alone; while many a light
Flared, here and there, from wealthy festivals,
And threw their moving shadows on the walls,
Or found them cluster'd in the corniced shade
Of some arch'd temple door, or dusky colonnade.

Muffling his face, of greeting friends in fear,
Her fingers he press'd hard, as one came near
With curl'd gray beard, sharp eyes, and smooth bald crown,
Slow-stepp'd, and robed in philosophic gown:
Lycius shrank closer, as they met and past,
Into his mantle, adding wings to haste,
While hurried Lamia trembled: "Ah," said he,
"Why do you shudder, love, so ruefully?
Why does your tender palm dissolve in dew?"—
"I'm wearied," said fair Lamia: "tell me who
Is that old man? I cannot bring to mind
His features—Lycius! wherefore did you blind
Yourself from his quick eyes?" Lycius replied,
'Tis Apollonius sage, my trusty guide
And good instructor; but to-night he seems
The ghost of folly haunting my sweet dreams.

While yet he spake they had arrived before
A pillar'd porch, with lofty portal door,
Where hung a silver lamp, whose phosphor glow
Reflected in the slabbed steps below,
Mild as a star in water; for so new,
And so unsullied was the marble hue,
So through the crystal polish, liquid fine,
Ran the dark veins, that none but feet divine
Could e'er have touch'd there. Sounds Aeolian
Breath'd from the hinges, as the ample span
Of the wide doors disclos'd a place unknown
Some time to any, but those two alone,
And a few Persian mutes, who that same year
Were seen about the markets: none knew where
They could inhabit; the most curious
Were foil'd, who watch'd to trace them to their house:
And but the flitter-winged verse must tell,
For truth's sake, what woe afterwards befel,
'Twould humour many a heart to leave them thus,
Shut from the busy world of more incredulous.

Part 2

Love in a hut, with water and a crust,
Is—Love, forgive us!—cinders, ashes, dust;
Love in a palace is perhaps at last
More grievous torment than a hermit's fast—
That is a doubtful tale from faery land,
Hard for the non-elect to understand.
Had Lycius liv'd to hand his story down,
He might have given the moral a fresh frown,
Or clench'd it quite: but too short was their bliss
To breed distrust and hate, that make the soft voice hiss.
Besides, there, nightly, with terrific glare,
Love, jealous grown of so complete a pair,
Hover'd and buzz'd his wings, with fearful roar,
Above the lintel of their chamber door,
And down the passage cast a glow upon the floor.
For all this came a ruin: side by side
They were enthroned, in the even tide,
Upon a couch, near to a curtaining
Whose airy texture, from a golden string,
Floated into the room, and let appear
Unveil'd the summer heaven, blue and clear,
Betwixt two marble shafts:—there they reposed,
Where use had made it sweet, with eyelids closed,
Saving a tythe which love still open kept,
That they might see each other while they almost slept;
When from the slope side of a suburb hill,
Deafening the swallow's twitter, came a thrill
Of trumpets—Lycius started—the sounds fled,
But left a thought, a buzzing in his head.

For the first time, since first he harbour'd in
That purple-lined palace of sweet sin,
His spirit pass'd beyond its golden bourn
Into the noisy world almost forsworn.
The lady, ever watchful, penetrant,
Saw this with pain, so arguing a want
Of something more, more than her empery
Of joys; and she began to moan and sigh
Because he mused beyond her, knowing well
That but a moment's thought is passion's passing bell.
"Why do you sigh, fair creature?" whisper'd he:
"Why do you think?" return'd she tenderly:
"You have deserted me—where am I now?
Not in your heart while care weighs on your brow:
No, no, you have dismiss'd me; and I go
From your breast houseless: ay, it must be so."
He answer'd, bending to her open eyes,
Where he was mirror'd small in paradise,
My silver planet, both of eve and morn!
Why will you plead yourself so sad forlorn,
While I am striving how to fill my heart
With deeper crimson, and a double smart?
How to entangle, trammel up and snare
Your soul in mine, and labyrinth you there
Like the hid scent in an unbudded rose?
Ay, a sweet kiss—you see your mighty woes.
My thoughts! shall I unveil them? Listen then!
What mortal hath a prize, that other men
May be confounded and abash'd withal,
But lets it sometimes pace abroad majestical,
And triumph, as in thee I should rejoice
Amid the hoarse alarm of Corinth's voice.

"Let my foes choke, and my friends shout afar,
While through the thronged streets your bridal car
Wheels round its dazzling spokes." The lady's cheek
Trembled; she nothing said, but, pale and meek,
Arose and knelt before him, wept a rain
Of sorrows at his words; at last with pain
Beseeching him, the while his hand she wrung,
To change his purpose. He thereat was stung,
Perverse, with stronger fancy to reclaim
Her wild and timid nature to his aim:
Besides, for all his love, in self despite,
Against his better self, he took delight
Luxurious in her sorrows, soft and new.
His passion, cruel grown, took on a hue
Fierce and sanguineous as 'twas possible
In one whose brow had no dark veins to swell.
Fine was the mitigated fury, like
Apollo's presence when in act to strike
The serpent—Ha, the serpent! certes, she
Was none. She burnt, she lov'd the tyranny,
And, all subdued, consented to the hour
When to the bridal he should lead his paramour.

Whispering in midnight silence, said the youth,
"Sure some sweet name thou hast, though, by my truth,
I have not ask'd it, ever thinking thee
Not mortal, but of heavenly progeny,
As still I do. Hast any mortal name,
Fit appellation for this dazzling frame?
Or friends or kinsfolk on the citied earth,
To share our marriage feast and nuptial mirth?"
"I have no friends," said Lamia," no, not one;
My presence in wide Corinth hardly known:
My parents' bones are in their dusty urns
Sepulchred, where no kindled incense burns,
Seeing all their luckless race are dead, save me,
And I neglect the holy rite for thee.
Even as you list invite your many guests;
But if, as now it seems, your vision rests
With any pleasure on me, do not bid
Old Apollonius—from him keep me hid."
Lycius, perplex'd at words so blind and blank,
Made close inquiry; from whose touch she shrank,
Feigning a sleep; and he to the dull shade
Of deep sleep in a moment was betray'd
It was the custom then to bring away
The bride from home at blushing shut of day,
Veil'd, in a chariot, heralded along
By strewn flowers, torches, and a marriage song,
With other pageants: but this fair unknown
Had not a friend. So being left alone,
(Lycius was gone to summon all his kin)
And knowing surely she could never win
His foolish heart from its mad pompousness,
She set herself, high-thoughted, how to dress
The misery in fit magnificence.

She did so, but 'tis doubtful how and whence
Came, and who were her subtle servitors.
About the halls, and to and from the doors,
There was a noise of wings, till in short space
The glowing banquet-room shone with wide-arched grace.
A haunting music, sole perhaps and lone
Supportress of the faery-roof, made moan
Throughout, as fearful the whole charm might fade.
Fresh carved cedar, mimicking a glade
Of palm and plantain, met from either side,
High in the midst, in honour of the bride:
Two palms and then two plantains, and so on,
From either side their stems branch'd one to one
All down the aisled place; and beneath all
There ran a stream of lamps straight on from wall to wall.
So canopied, lay an untasted feast
Teeming with odours. Lamia, regal drest,
Silently paced about, and as she went,
In pale contented sort of discontent,
Mission'd her viewless servants to enrich
The fretted splendour of each nook and niche.
Between the tree-stems, marbled plain at first,
Came jasper pannels; then, anon, there burst
Forth creeping imagery of slighter trees,
And with the larger wove in small intricacies.
Approving all, she faded at self-will,
And shut the chamber up, close, hush'd and still,
Complete and ready for the revels rude,
When dreadful guests would come to spoil her solitude.

The day appear'd, and all the gossip rout.
O senseless Lycius! Madman! wherefore flout
The silent-blessing fate, warm cloister'd hours,
And show to common eyes these secret bowers?
The herd approach'd; each guest, with busy brain,
Arriving at the portal, gaz'd amain,
And enter'd marveling: for they knew the street,
Remember'd it from childhood all complete
Without a gap, yet ne'er before had seen
That royal porch, that high-built fair demesne;
So in they hurried all, maz'd, curious and keen:
Save one, who look'd thereon with eye severe,
And with calm-planted steps walk'd in austere;
'Twas Apollonius: something too he laugh'd,
As though some knotty problem, that had daft
His patient thought, had now begun to thaw,
And solve and melt—'twas just as he foresaw.
He met within the murmurous vestibule
His young disciple. "'Tis no common rule,
Lycius," said he, "for uninvited guest
To force himself upon you, and infest
With an unbidden presence the bright throng
Of younger friends; yet must I do this wrong,
And you forgive me." Lycius blush'd, and led
The old man through the inner doors broad-spread;
With reconciling words and courteous mien
Turning into sweet milk the sophist's spleen.

Of wealthy lustre was the banquet-room,
Fill'd with pervading brilliance and perfume:
Before each lucid pannel fuming stood
A censer fed with myrrh and spiced wood,
Each by a sacred tripod held aloft,
Whose slender feet wide-swerv'd upon the soft
Wool-woofed carpets: fifty wreaths of smoke
From fifty censers their light voyage took
To the high roof, still mimick'd as they rose
Along the mirror'd walls by twin-clouds odorous.
Twelve sphered tables, by silk seats insphered,
High as the level of a man's breast rear'd
On libbard's paws, upheld the heavy gold
Of cups and goblets, and the store thrice told
Of Ceres' horn, and, in huge vessels, wine
Come from the gloomy tun with merry shine.
Thus loaded with a feast the tables stood,
Each shrining in the midst the image of a God.
When in an antichamber every guest
Had felt the cold full sponge to pleasure press'd,
By minist'ring slaves, upon his hands and feet,
And fragrant oils with ceremony meet
Pour'd on his hair, they all mov'd to the feast
In white robes, and themselves in order placed
Around the silken couches, wondering
Whence all this mighty cost and blaze of wealth could
spring.

Soft went the music the soft air along,
While fluent Greek a vowel'd undersong
Kept up among the guests discoursing low
At first, for scarcely was the wine at flow;
But when the happy vintage touch'd their brains,
Louder they talk, and louder come the strains
Of powerful instruments—the gorgeous dyes,
The space, the splendour of the draperies,
The roof of awful richness, nectarous cheer,
Beautiful slaves, and Lamia's self, appear,
Now, when the wine has done its rosy deed,
And every soul from human trammels freed,
No more so strange; for merry wine, sweet wine,
Will make Elysian shades not too fair, too divine.
Soon was God Bacchus at meridian height;
Flush'd were their cheeks, and bright eyes double bright:
Garlands of every green, and every scent
From vales deflower'd, or forest-trees branch rent,
In baskets of bright osier'd gold were brought
High as the handles heap'd, to suit the thought
Of every guest; that each, as he did please,
Might fancy-fit his brows, silk-pillow'd at his ease.
What wreath for Lamia? What for Lycius?
What for the sage, old Apollonius?
Upon her aching forehead be there hung
The leaves of willow and of adder's tongue;
And for the youth, quick, let us strip for him
The thyrsus, that his watching eyes may swim
Into forgetfulness; and, for the sage,
Let spear-grass and the spiteful thistle wage
War on his temples. Do not all charms fly
At the mere touch of cold philosophy?

There was an awful rainbow once in heaven:
We know her woof, her texture; she is given
In the dull catalogue of common things.
Philosophy will clip an Angel's wings,
Conquer all mysteries by rule and line,
Empty the haunted air, and gnomed mine—
Unweave a rainbow, as it erewhile made
The tender-person'd Lamia melt into a shade.
By her glad Lycius sitting, in chief place,
Scarce saw in all the room another face,
Till, checking his love trance, a cup he took
Full brimm'd, and opposite sent forth a look
'Cross the broad table, to beseech a glance
From his old teacher's wrinkled countenance,
And pledge him. The bald-head philosopher
Had fix'd his eye, without a twinkle or stir
Full on the alarmed beauty of the bride,
Brow-beating her fair form, and troubling her sweet pride.
Lycius then press'd her hand, with devout touch,
As pale it lay upon the rosy couch:
'Twas icy, and the cold ran through his veins;
Then sudden it grew hot, and all the pains
Of an unnatural heat shot to his heart.
"Lamia, what means this? Wherefore dost thou start?
Know'st thou that man?" Poor Lamia answer'd not.
He gaz'd into her eyes, and not a jot
Own'd they the lovelorn piteous appeal:
More, more he gaz'd: his human senses reel:
Some hungry spell that loveliness absorbs;
There was no recognition in those orbs.

"Lamia!" he cried—and no soft-toned reply.
The many heard, and the loud revelry
Grew hush; the stately music no more breathes;
The myrtle sicken'd in a thousand wreaths.
By faint degrees, voice, lute, and pleasure ceased;
A deadly silence step by step increased,
Until it seem'd a horrid presence there,
And not a man but felt the terror in his hair.
"Lamia!" he shriek'd; and nothing but the shriek
With its sad echo did the silence break.
"Begone, foul dream!" he cried, gazing again
In the bride's face, where now no azure vein
Wander'd on fair-spaced temples; no soft bloom
Misted the cheek; no passion to illume
The deep-recessed vision—all was blight;
Lamia, no longer fair, there sat a deadly white.
"Shut, shut those juggling eyes, thou ruthless man!
Turn them aside, wretch! or the righteous ban
Of all the Gods, whose dreadful images
Here represent their shadowy presences,
May pierce them on the sudden with the thorn
Of painful blindness; leaving thee forlorn,
In trembling dotage to the feeblest fright
Of conscience, for their long offended might,
For all thine impious proud-heart sophistries,
Unlawful magic, and enticing lies.

Corinthians! look upon that gray-beard wretch!
Mark how, possess'd, his lashless eyelids stretch
Around his demon eyes! Corinthians, see!
My sweet bride withers at their potency."
"Fool!" said the sophist, in an under-tone
Gruff with contempt; which a death-nighing moan
From Lycius answer'd, as heart-struck and lost,
He sank supine beside the aching ghost.
"Fool! Fool!" repeated he, while his eyes still
Relented not, nor mov'd; "from every ill
Of life have I preserv'd thee to this day,
And shall I see thee made a serpent's prey?"
Then Lamia breath'd death breath; the sophist's eye,
Like a sharp spear, went through her utterly,
Keen, cruel, perceant, stinging: she, as well
As her weak hand could any meaning tell,
Motion'd him to be silent; vainly so,
He look'd and look'd again a level—No!
"A Serpent!" echoed he; no sooner said,
Than with a frightful scream she vanished:
And Lycius' arms were empty of delight,
As were his limbs of life, from that same night.
On the high couch he lay!—his friends came round
Supported him—no pulse, or breath they found,
And, in its marriage robe, the heavy body wound.

The Vampire
Conrad Aiken

VAMPIRES IN LITERATURE

She rose among us where we lay.
She wept, we put our work away.
She chilled our laughter, stilled our play;
And spread a silence there.
And darkness shot across the sky,
And once, and twice, we heard her cry;
And saw her lift white hands on high
And toss her troubled hair.

What shape was this who came to us,
With basilisk eyes so ominous,
With mouth so sweet, so poisonous,
And tortured hands so pale?
We saw her wavering to and fro,
Through dark and wind we saw her go;
Yet what her name was did not know;
And felt our spirits fail.

We tried to turn away; but still
Above we heard her sorrow thrill;
And those that slept, they dreamed of ill
And dreadful things:
Of skies grown red with rending flames
And shuddering hills that cracked their frames;
Of twilights foul with wings;

And skeletons dancing to a tune;
And cries of children stifled soon;
And over all a blood-red moon
A dull and nightmare size.
They woke, and sought to go their ways,

Yet everywhere they met her gaze,
Her fixed and burning eyes.

Who are you now, —we cried to her—
Spirit so strange, so sinister?
We felt dead winds above us stir;
And in the darkness heard
A voice fall, singing, cloying sweet,
Heavily dropping, though that heat,
Heavy as honeyed pulses beat,
Slow word by anguished word.

And through the night strange music went
With voice and cry so darkly blent
We could not fathom what they meant;
Save only that they seemed
To thin the blood along our veins,
Foretelling vile, delirious pains,
And clouds divulging blood-red rains
Upon a hill undreamed.

And this we heard: "Who dies for me,
He shall possess me secretly,
My terrible beauty he shall see,
And slake my body's flame.
But who denies me cursed shall be,
And slain, and buried loathsomely,
And slimed upon with shame."

And darkness fell. And like a sea
Of stumbling deaths we followed, we

Who dared not stay behind.
There all night long beneath a cloud
We rose and fell, we struck and bowed,
We were the ploughman and the ploughed,
Our eyes were red and blind.

And some, they said, had touched her side,
Before she fled us there;
And some had taken her to bride;
And some lain down for her and died;
Who had not touched her hair,
Ran to and fro and cursed and cried
And sought her everywhere.

"Her eyes have feasted on the dead,
And small and shapely is her head,
And dark and small her mouth," they said,
"And beautiful to kiss;
Her mouth is sinister and red
As blood in moonlight is."

Then poets forgot their jeweled words
And cut the sky with glittering swords;
And innocent souls turned carrion birds
To perch upon the dead.
Sweet daisy fields were drenched with death,
The air became a charnel breath,
Pale stones were splashed with red.

Green leaves were dappled bright with blood
And fruit trees murdered in the bud;

And when at length the dawn
Came green as twilight from the east,
And all that heaving horror ceased,
Silent was every bird and beast,
And that dark voice was gone.

No word was there, no song, no bell,
No furious tongue that dream to tell;
Only the dead, who rose and fell
Above the wounded men;
And whisperings and wails of pain
Blown slowly from the wounded grain,
Blown slowly from the smoking plain;
And silence fallen again.

Until at dusk, from God knows where,
Beneath dark birds that filled the air,
Like one who did not hear or care,
Under a blood-red cloud,
An aged ploughman came alone
And drove his share through flesh and bone,
And turned them under to mould and stone;
All night long he ploughed.

The Vampire Bride
Henry Thomas Liddell

"I am come—I am come! once again from the tomb,
In return for the ring which you gave;
That I am thine, and that thou art mine,
This nuptial pledge receive."

He lay like a corse 'neath the Demon's force,
And she wrapp'd him in a shroud;
And she fixed her teeth his heart beneath,
And she drank of the warm life-blood!

And ever and anon murmur'd the lips of stone,
"Soft and warm is this couch of thine,
Thou'lt to-morrow be laid on a colder bed—
Albert! that bed will be mine!"

Christabel
Samuel Taylor Coleridge

(This work was stopped after 2 parts and never completed.)

"Come back into memory, like as thou wert in the day spring of thy fancies, with hope like a fiery column before thee—the dark pillar not yet turned—Samuel Taylor Coleridge—Logician, Metaphysician, Bard!"

ESSAYS OF ELIA

Part The First

'Tis the middle of night by the castle clock,
And the owls have awakened the crowing cock,"
Tu—whit!—Tu—whoo!
And hark, again! the crowing cock,
How drowsily it crew.

Sir Leoline; the Baron rich,
Hath a toothless mastiff, which
From her kennel beneath the rock
Maketh answer to the clock,
Four for the quarters, and twelve for the hour;
Ever and aye, by shine and shower,
Sixteen short howls, not over loud;
Some say, she sees my lady's shroud.

Is the night chilly and dark?
The night is chilly, but not dark.
The thin gray cloud is spread on high,
It covers but not hides the sky.
The moon is behind, and at the full;
And yet she looks both small and dull.
The night is chill, the cloud is gray:
'Tis a month before the month of May,
And the Spring comes slowly up this way.

The lovely lady, Christabel,
Whom her father loves so well,
What makes her in the wood so late,

VAMPIRES IN LITERATURE

A furlong from the castle gate?
She had dreams all yesternight
Of her own betrothed knight;
And she in the midnight wood will pray
For the weal of her lover that's far away.

She stole along, she nothing spoke,
The sighs she heaved were soft and low,
And naught was green upon the oak
But moss and rarest misletoe:
She kneels beneath the huge oak tree,
And in silence prayeth she.

The lady sprang up suddenly,
The lovely lady, Christabel!
It moaned as near, as near can be,
But what it is she cannot tell.—
On the other side it seems to be,
Of the huge, broad-breasted, old oak tree.

The night is chill; the forest bare;
Is it the wind that moaneth bleak?
There is not wind enough in the air
To move away the ringlet curl
From the lovely lady's cheek—
There is not wind enough to twirl
The one red leaf, the last of its clan,
That dances as often as dance it can,
Hanging so light, and hanging so high,
On the topmost twig that looks up at the sky.

Hush, beating heart of Christabel!
Jesu, Maria, shield her well!

She folded her arms beneath her cloak,
And stole to the other side of the oak.
What sees she there?

There she sees a damsel bright,
Drest in a silken robe of white,
That shadowy in the moonlight shone:
The neck that made that white robe wan,
Her stately neck, and arms were bare;
Her blue-veined feet unsandal'd were,
And wildly glittered here and there
The gems entangled in her hair.
I guess, 'twas frightful there to see
A lady so richly clad as she—
Beautiful exceedingly!

Mary mother, save me now!
(Said Christabel,) And who art thou?

The lady strange made answer meet,
And her voice was faint and sweet:—
Have pity on my sore distress,
I scarce can speak for weariness:
Stretch forth thy hand, and have no fear!
Said Christabel, How camest thou here?
And the lady, whose voice was faint and sweet,
Did thus pursue her answer meet:—

My sire is of a noble line,
And my name is Geraldine:
Five warriors seized me yestermorn,
Me, even me, a maid forlorn:
They choked my cries with force and fright,

And tied me on a palfrey white.

The palfrey was as fleet as wind,
And they rode furiously behind.
They spurred amain, their steeds were white:
And once we crossed the shade of night.
As sure as Heaven shall rescue me,
I have no thought what men they be;
Nor do I know how long it is
(For I have lain entranced I wis)
Since one, the tallest of the five,
Took me from the palfrey's back,
A weary woman, scarce alive.
Some muttered words his comrades spoke:
He placed me underneath this oak;
He swore they would return with haste;
Whither they went I cannot tell
I thought I heard, some minutes past,
Sounds as of a castle bell.
Stretch forth thy hand (thus ended she),
And help a wretched maid to flee.

Then Christabel stretched forth her hand,
And comforted fair Geraldine:
O well, bright dame! may you command
The service of Sir Leoline;
And gladly our stout chivalry
Will he send forth and friends withal
To guide and guard you safe and free
Home to your noble father's hall.

She rose: and forth with steps they passed
That strove to be, and were not, fast.

Her gracious stars the lady blest,
And thus spake on sweet Christabel:
All our household are at rest,
The hall as silent as the cell;
Sir Leoline is weak in health,
And may not well awakened be,
But we will move as if in stealth,
And I beseech your courtesy,
This night, to share your couch with me.

They crossed the moat, and Christabel
Took the key that fitted well;
A little door she opened straight,
All in the middle of the gate;
The gate that was ironed within and without
Where an army in battle array had marched out.
The lady sank, belike through pain,
And Christabel with might and main
Lifted her up, a weary weight,
Over the threshold of the gate:
Then the lady rose again,
And moved, as she were not in pain.

So free from danger, free from fear,
They crossed the court: right glad they were.
And Christabel devoutly cried
To the lady by her side,
Praise we the Virgin all divine
Who hath rescued thee from thy distress!
Alas! alas! said Geraldine,
I cannot speak for weariness.
So free from danger, free from fear,

VAMPIRES IN LITERATURE

They crossed the court: right glad they were.

Outside her kennel, the mastiff old
Lay fast asleep, in moonshine cold.
The mastiff old did not awake,
Yet she an angry moan did make!
And what can ail the mastiff bitch?
Never till now she uttered yell
Beneath the eye of Christabel.
Perhaps it is the owlet's scritch:
For what can ail the mastiff bitch?

They passed the hall, that echoes still,
Pass as lightly as you will!
The brands were flat, the brands were dying,
Amid their own white ashes lying;
But when the lady passed, there came
A tongue of light, a fit of flame
And Christabel saw the lady's eye,
And nothing else saw she thereby,
Save the boss of the shield of Sir Leoline tall,
Which hung in a murky old niche in the wall.
O softly tread, said Christabel,
My father seldom sleepeth well.

Sweet Christabel her feet doth bare,
And jealous of the listening air
They steal their way from stair to stair,
Now in glimmer, and now in gloom,
And now they pass the Baron's room,
As still as death with stifled breath!
And now have reached her chamber door;
And now doth Geraldine press down

VAMPIRES IN LITERATURE

The rushes of the chamber floor.

The moon shines dim in the open air,
And not a moonbeam enters here.
But they without its light can see
The chamber carved so curiously,
Carved with figures strange and sweet,
All made out of the carver's brain,
For a lady's chamber meet:
The lamp with twofold silver chain
Is fastened to an angel's feet.

The silver lamp burns dead and dim;
But Christabel the lamp will trim.
She trimmed the lamp, and made it bright,
And left it swinging to and fro,
While Geraldine, in wretched plight,
Sank down upon the floor below.

O weary lady, Geraldine,
I pray you, drink this cordial wine!
It is a wine of virtuous powers;
My mother made it of wild flowers.
And will your mother pity me,
Who am a maiden most forlorn?
Christabel answered—Woe is me!
She died the hour that I was born.
I have heard the grey-haired friar tell
How on her death-bed she did say,
That she should hear the castle-bell
Strike twelve upon my wedding-day.
O mother dear! that thou wert here!
I would, said Geraldine, she were!

But soon with altered voice, said she—
"Off, wandering mother! Peak and pine!
I have power to bid thee flee."
Alas! what ails poor Geraldine?
Why stares she with unsettled eye?
Can she the bodiless dead espy?
And why with hollow voice cries she,
"Off, woman, off! this hour is mine—
Though thou her guardian spirit be,
Off, woman, off! 'tis given to me."

Then Christabel knelt by the lady's side,
And raised to heaven her eyes so blue—,
Alas! said she, this ghastly ride—
Dear lady! it hath wildered you!
The lady wiped her moist cold brow,
And faintly said, "'tis over now!"
Again the wild-flower wine she drank:
Her fair large eyes 'gan glitter bright,
And from the floor whereon she sank,
The lofty lady stood upright:
She was most beautiful to see,
Like a lady of a far countrée.
And thus the lofty lady spake—
"All they who live in the upper sky,
Do love you, holy Christabel!
And you love them, and for their sake
And for the good which me befel,
Even I in my degree will try,
Fair maiden, to requite you well.
But now unrobe yourself; for I
Must pray, ere yet in bed I lie."

Quoth Christabel, So let it be!
And as the lady bade, did she.
Her gentle limbs did she undress,
And lay down in her loveliness.

But through her brain of weal and woe
So many thoughts moved to and fro,
That vain it were her lids to close;
So half-way from the bed she rose,
And on her elbow did recline
To look at the lady Geraldine.

Beneath the lamp the lady bowed,
And slowly rolled her eyes around
Then drawing in her breath aloud,
Like one that shuddered, she unbound
The cincture from beneath her breast:
Her silken robe, and inner vest,
Dropt to her feet, and full in view,
Behold! her bosom and half her side———
A sight to dream of, not to tell!
O shield her! shield sweet Christabel!

Yet Geraldine nor speaks nor stirs;
Ah! what a stricken look was hers!
Deep from within she seems half-way
To lift some weight with sick assay,
And eyes the maid and seeks delay;
Then suddenly, as one defied,
Collects herself in scorn and pride,
And lay down by the Maiden's side!—
And in her arms the maid she took,

Ah wel-a-day!
And with low voice and doleful look

These words did say:
In the touch of this bosom there worketh a spell,
Which is lord of thy utterance, Christabel!
Thou knowest to-night, and wilt know to-morrow,
This mark of my shame, this seal of my sorrow;
But vainly thou warrest,
For his is alone in
Thy power to declare,
That in the dim forest
Thou heard'st a low moaning,
And found'st a bright lady, surpassingly fair;
And didst bring her home with thee in love and in charity,
To shield her and shelter her from the damp air."

THE CONCLUSION TO PART THE FIRST
It was a lovely sight to see
The lady Christabel, when she
Was praying at the old oak tree.
Amid the jagged shadows
Of mossy leafless boughs,
Kneeling in the moonlight,
To make her gentle vows;
Her slender palms together prest,
Heaving sometimes on her breast;
Her face resigned to bliss or bale—
Her face, oh call it fair not pale,
And both blue eyes more, bright than clear,
Each about to have a tear.

With open eyes (ah woe is me!)
Asleep, and dreaming fearfully,
Fearfully dreaming, yet, I wis,.

Dreaming that alone, which is—
O sorrow and shame! Can this be she,
The lady, who knelt at the old oak tree?
And lo! the worker of these harms,
That holds the maiden in her arms,
Seems to slumber still and mild,
As a mother with her child.

A star hath set, a star hath risen,
O Geraldine! since arms of thine
Have been the lovely lady's prison.
O Geraldine! one hour was thine
Thou'st had thy will! By tairn and rill,
The night-birds all that hour were still.
But now they are jubilant anew,
From cliff and tower, tu-whoo! tu-whoo!
Tu-whoo! tu-whoo! from wood and fell!

And see! the lady Christabel
Gathers herself from out her trance;
Her limbs relax, her countenance
Grows sad and soft; the smooth thin lids
Close o'er her eyes; and tears she sheds
Large tears that leave the lashes bright!
And oft the while she seems to smile
As infants at a sudden light!

Yea, she doth smile, and she doth weep,
Like a youthful hermitess,

Beauteous in a wilderness,
Who, praying always, prays in sleep.
And, if she move unquietly,
Perchance, 'tis but the blood so free

Comes back and tingles in her feet.
No doubt, she hath a vision sweet.
What if her guardian spirit 'twere,
What if she knew her mother near?
But this she knows, in joys and woes,
That saints will aid if men will call:
For the blue sky bends over all!

The Blue Fairy Book (1891), ed. Andrew Lang;
illus. H. J. Ford and Lancelot Speed

Part The Second

Each matin bell, the Baron saith,
Knells us back to a world of death.
These words Sir Leoline first said,
When he rose and found his lady dead:
These words Sir Leoline will say
Many a morn to his dying day!

And hence the custom and law began
That still at dawn the sacristan,
Who duly pulls the heavy bell,
Five and forty beads must tell
Between each stroke—a warning knell,
Which not a soul can choose but hear
From Bratha Head to Wyndermere.
Saith Bracy the bard, So let it knell!
And let the drowsy sacristan
Still count as slowly as he can!
There is no lack of such, I ween,
As well fill up the space between.
In Langdale Pike and Witch's Lair,
And Dungeon-ghyll so foully rent,
With ropes of rock and bells of air
Three sinful sextons' ghosts are pent,
Who all give back, one after t'other,
The death-note to their living brother;
And oft too, by the knell offended,
Just as their one! two! three! is ended,
The devil mocks the doleful tale
With a merry peal from Borrowdale.

The air is still! through mist and cloud
That merry peal comes ringing loud;
And Geraldine shakes off her dread,
And rises lightly from the bed;
Puts on her silken vestments white,
And tricks her hair in lovely plight,
And nothing doubting of her spell
Awakens the lady Christabel
"Sleep you, sweet lady Christabel?
I trust that you have rested well."

And Christabel awoke and spied
The same who lay down by her side—
O rather say, the same whom she
Raised up beneath the old oak tree!
Nay, fairer yet! and yet more fair!
For she belike hath drunken deep
Of all the blessedness of sleep!
And while she spake, her looks, her air,
Such gentle thankfulness declare,
That (so it seemed) her girded vests
Grew tight beneath her heaving breasts.
"Sure I have sinn'd!" said Christabel,
"Now heaven be praised if all be well!"
And in low faltering tones, yet sweet,
Did she the lofty lady greet
With such perplexity of mind
As dreams too lively leave behind.

So quickly she rose, and quickly arrayed
Her maiden limbs, and having prayed
That He, who on the cross did groan,
Might wash away her sins unknown,

She forthwith led fair Geraldine
To meet her sire, Sir Leoline.

The lovely maid and the lady tall
Are pacing both into the hall,
And pacing on through page and groom,
Enter the Baron's presence-room.

The Baron rose, and while he prest
His gentle daughter to his breast,
With cheerful wonder in his eyes
The lady Geraldine espies,
And gave such welcome to the same,
As might beseem so bright a dame!

But when he heard the lady's tale,
And when she told her father's name,
Why waxed Sir Leoline so pale,
Murmuring o'er the name again,
Lord Roland de Vaux of Tryermaine?

Alas! they had been friends in youth;
But whispering tongues can poison truth;
And constancy lives in realms above;
And life is thorny; and youth is vain;
And to be wroth with one we love
Doth work like madness in the brain.
And thus it chanced, as I divine,
With Roland and Sir Leoline.
Each spake words of high disdain
And insult to his heart's best brother:
They parted—ne'er to meet again!
But never either found another

To free the hollow heart from paining—
They stood aloof, the scars remaining,
Like cliffs which had been rent asunder;
A dreary sea now flows between.
But neither heat, nor frost, nor thunder,
Shall wholly do away, I ween,
The marks of that which once hath been.
Sir Leoline, a moment's space,
Stood gazing on the damsel's face:
And the youthful Lord of Tryermaine
Came back upon his heart again.

O then the Baron forgot his age,
His noble heart swelled high with rage;
He swore by the wounds in Jesu's side
He would proclaim it far and wide,
With trump and solemn heraldry,
That they, who thus had wronged the dame
Were base as spotted infamy!
"And if they dare deny the same,
My herald shall appoint a week,
And let the recreant traitors seek
My tourney court—that there and then
I may dislodge their reptile souls
From the bodies and forms of men!"
He spake: his eye in lightning rolls!
For the lady was ruthlessly seized; and he kenned
In the beautiful lady the child of his friend!

And now the tears were on his face,
And fondly in his arms he took
Fair Geraldine, who met the embrace,

Prolonging it with joyous look.
Which when she viewed, a vision fell
Upon the soul of Christabel,

The vision of fear, the touch and pain!
She shrunk and shuddered, and saw again—
(Ah, woe is me! Was it for thee,
Thou gentle maid! such sights to see?)

Again she saw that bosom old,
Again she felt that bosom cold,
And drew in her breath with a hissing sound:
Whereat the Knight turned wildly round,
And nothing saw, but his own sweet maid
With eyes upraised, as one that prayed.

The touch, the sight, had passed away,
And in its stead that vision blest,
Which comforted her after-rest,
While in the lady's arms she lay,
Had put a rapture in her breast,
And on her lips and o'er her eyes
Spread smiles like light!

With new surprise,
"What ails then my beloved child?"
The Baron said—His daughter mild
Made answer, "All will yet be well!"
I ween, she had no power to tell
Aught else: so mighty was the spell.
Yet he, who saw this Geraldine,
Had deemed her sure a thing divine.
Such sorrow with such grace she blended,

As if she feared she had offended

Sweet Christabel, that gentle maid!
And with such lowly tones she prayed
She might be sent without delay
Home to her father's mansion.

"Nay!
Nay, by my soul!" said Leoline.
"Ho! Bracy the bard, the charge be thine!
Go thou, with music sweet and loud,
And take two steeds with trappings proud,
And take the youth whom thou lov'st best
To bear thy harp, and learn thy song,
And clothe you both in solemn vest,
And over the mountains haste along,
Lest wandering folk, that are abroad,
Detain you on the valley road.

"And when he has crossed the Irthing flood,
My merry bard! he hastes, he hastes
Up Knorren Moor, through Halegarth Wood,
And reaches soon that castle good
Which stands and threatens Scotland's wastes.

"Bard Bracy! bard Bracy! your horses are fleet,
Ye must ride up the hall, your music so sweet,
More loud than your horses' echoing feet!
And loud and loud to Lord Roland call,
Thy daughter is safe in Langdale hall!
Thy beautiful daughter is safe and free—
Sir Leoline greets thee thus through me.

He bids thee come without delay
With all thy numerous array;
And take thy lovely daughter home:
And he will meet thee on the way
With all his numerous array
White with their panting palfreys' foam:
And, by mine honour! I will say,
That I repent me of the day
When I spake words of fierce disdain
To Roland de Vaux of Tryermaine!—
—For since that evil hour hath flown,
Many a summer's sun hath shone;
Yet ne'er found I a friend again
Like Roland de Vaux of Tryermaine."

The lady fell, and clasped his knees,
Her face upraised, her eyes o'erflowing;
And Bracy replied, with faltering voice,
His gracious hail on all bestowing;
"Thy words, thou sire of Christabel,
Are sweeter than my harp can tell;
Yet might I gain a boon of thee,
This day my journey should not be,
So strange a dream hath come to me;
That I had vowed with music loud
To clear yon wood from thing unblest,
Warn'd by a vision in my rest!
For in my sleep I saw that dove,
That gentle bird, whom thou dost love,
And call'st by thy own daughter's name—
Sir Leoline! I saw the same,
Fluttering, and uttering fearful moan,
Among the green herbs in the forest alone.

Which when I saw and when I heard,
I wonder'd what might ail the bird;
For nothing near it could I see,
Save the grass and green herbs underneath the old tree.
"And in my dream, methought, I went
To search out what might there be found;
And what the sweet bird's trouble meant,
That thus lay fluttering on the ground.
I went and peered, and could descry
No cause for her distressful cry;
But yet for her dear lady's sake
I stooped, methought, the dove to take,
When lo! I saw a bright green snake
Coiled around its wings and neck.
Green as the herbs on which it couched,
Close by the dove's its head it crouched;
And with the dove it heaves and stirs,
Swelling its neck as she swelled hers!
I woke; it was the midnight hour,
The clock was echoing in the tower;
But though my slumber was gone by,
This dream it would not pass away—
It seems to live upon my eye!
And thence I vowed this self-same day
With music strong and saintly song
To wander through the forest bare,
Lest aught unholy loiter there."
Thus Bracy said: the Baron, the while,
Half-listening heard him with a smile;
Then turned to Lady Geraldine,
His eyes made up of wonder and love;
And said in courtly accents fine,
"Sweet maid, Lord Roland's beauteous dove,

With arms more strong than harp or song,
Thy sire and I will crush the snake!"
He kissed her forehead as he spake,
And Geraldine in maiden wise
Casting down her large bright eyes,
With blushing cheek and courtesy fine
She turned her from Sir Leoline;
Softly gathering up her train,
That o'er her right arm fell again;
And folded her arms across her chest,
And couched her head upon her breast,
And looked askance at Christabel—
Jesu, Maria, shield her well!

A snake's small eye blinks dull and shy,
And the lady's eyes they shrunk in her head,
Each shrunk up to a serpent's eye,
And with somewhat of malice, and more of dread,
At Christabel she look'd askance!—
One moment—and the sight was fled!
But Christabel in dizzy trance
Stumbling on the unsteady ground
Shuddered aloud, with a hissing sound;
And Geraldine again turned round,
And like a thing, that sought relief,
Full of wonder and full of grief,
She rolled her large bright eyes divine
Wildly on Sir Leoline.

The maid, alas! her thoughts are gone,
She nothing sees—no sight but one!
The maid, devoid of guile and sin,
I know not how, in fearful wise,

So deeply had she drunken in

That look, those shrunken serpent eyes,
That all her features were resigned
To this sole image in her mind:
And passively did imitate
That look of dull and treacherous hate!
And thus she stood, in dizzy trance,
Still picturing that look askance
With forced unconscious sympathy
Full before her father's view—
As far as such a look could be
In eyes so innocent and blue!

And when the trance was o'er, the maid
Paused awhile, and inly prayed:
Then falling at the Baron's feet,
"By my mother's soul do I entreat
That thou this woman send away!"
She said: and more she could not say:
For what she knew she could not tell,
O'er-mastered by the mighty spell.

Why is thy cheek so wan and wild,
Sir Leoline? Thy only child
Lies at thy feet, thy joy, thy pride,
So fair, so innocent, so mild;
The same, for whom thy lady died!
O, by the pangs of her dear mother
Think thou no evil of thy child!
For her, and thee, and for no other,
She prayed the moment ere she died:
Prayed that the babe for whom she died,

Might prove her dear lord's joy and pride!
That prayer her deadly pangs beguiled,
Sir Leoline!
And wouldst thou wrong thy only child,
Her child and thine?

Within the Baron's heart and brain
If thoughts, like these, had any share,
They only swelled his rage and pain,
And did but work confusion there.
His heart was cleft with pain and rage,
His cheeks they quivered, his eyes were wild,
Dishonour'd thus in his old age;
Dishonour'd by his only child,
And all his hospitality
To the insulted daughter of his friend
By more than woman's jealousy
Brought thus to a disgraceful end—
He rolled his eye with stern regard
Upon the gentle minstrel bard,
And said in tones abrupt, austere—
"Why, Bracy! dost thou loiter here?

I bade thee hence!" The bard obeyed;
And turning from his own sweet maid,
The aged knight, Sir Leoline,
Led forth the lady Geraldine!

THE CONCLUSION TO PART THE SECOND
A little child, a limber elf,
Singing, dancing to itself,
A fairy thing with red round cheeks,

That always finds, and never seeks,
Makes such a vision to the sight
As fills a father's eyes with light;
And pleasures flow in so thick and fast
Upon his heart, that he at last
Must needs express his love's excess
With words of unmeant bitterness.
Perhaps 'tis pretty to force together
Thoughts so all unlike each other;
To mutter and mock a broken charm,
To dally with wrong that does no harm.
Perhaps 'tis tender too and pretty
At each wild word to feel within
A sweet recoil of love and pity.
And what, if in a world of sin
(O sorrow and shame should this be true!)
Such giddiness of heart and brain
Comes seldom save from rage and pain,
So talks as it's most used to do.

The Giaour
Lord Byron

"One fatal remembrance—one sorrow that throws
It's bleak shade alike o'er our joys and our woes—
To which Life nothing brighter nor darker can bring,
For which joy hath no balm—and affliction no sting."

-Moore

TO:

SAMUEL ROGERS, ESQ.

AS A SLIGHT BUT MOST SINCERE TOKEN OF MY
ADMIRATION OF HIS GENIUS; MY RESPECT FOR
HIS CHARACTER, AND GRATITUDE FOR HIS
FRIENDSHIP; THIS PRODUCTION IS INSCRIBED
BY HIS OBLIGED AND AFFECTIONATE SERVANT,

-BYRON.

The Giaour

No breath of air to break the wave
That rolls below the Athenian's grave,
That tomb which, gleaming o'er the cliff,
First greets the homeward-veering skiff,
High o'er the land he saved in vain—
When shall such hero live again?

Far, dark, along the blue sea glancing,
The shadows of the rocks advancing,
Start on the fisher's eye like boat
Of island-pirate or Mainote;
And fearful for his light caique
He shuns the near but doubtful creek,
Though worn and weary with his toil,
And cumber'd with his scaly spoil,
Slowly, yet strongly, plies the oar,
Till Port Leone's safer shore
Receives him by the lovely light
That best becomes an Eastern night.

Who thundering comes on blackest steed?
With slacken'd bit and hoof of speed,
Beneath the clattering iron's sound
The cavern'd echoes wake around
In lash for lash, and bound for bound;
The foam that streaks the courser's side,
Seems gather'd from the ocean-tide:

Though weary waves are sunk to rest,
There's none within his rider's breast,
And though to-morrow's tempest lower,

'Tis calmer than thy heart, young Giaour
I know thee not, I loathe thy race,
But in thy lineaments I trace
What time shall strengthen, not efface;
Though young and pale, that sallow front
Is scath'd by fiery passion's brunt,
Though bent on earth thine evil eye
As meteor like thou glidest by,
Right well I view, and deem thee one
Whom Othman's sons should slay or shun.

The hour is past, the Giaour is gone,
But neither fled, nor fell alone;
Woe to that hour he came or went,
The curse for Hassan's sin was sent
To turn a palace to a tomb;
He came, he went, like the Simoom
That harbinger of fate and gloom,
Beneath whose widely-wasting breath
The very cypress droops to death—
Dark tree—still sad, when others' grief is fled,
The only constant mourner o'er the dead!

I hear the sound of coming feet,
But not a voice mine ear to greet—
More near—each turban I can scan,
And silver-sheathed ataghan
The foremost of the band is seen
An Emir by his garb of green

"Ho! who art thou?—this low salam
"Replies of Moslem faith I am."
"The burthen ye so gently bear,
"Seems one that claims your utmost care,
"And, doubtless, holds some precious freight,
"My humble bark would gladly wait.

"Thou speakest sooth, thy skiff unmoor,
"And waft us from the silent shore;
"Nay, leave the sail still furl'd, and ply
"The nearest oar that's scatter'd by,
"And midway to those rocks where sleep
"The channel'd waters dark and deep.—
"Rest from your task—so—bravely done,
"Our course has been right swiftly run,
"Yet 'tis the longest voyage, I trow,
"That one—

Sullen it plunged, and slowly sank,
The calm wave rippled to the bank;
I watch'd it as it sank, methought
Some motion from the current caught
Bestirr'd it more,—'twas but the beam
That checquer'd o'er the living stream—
I gaz'd, till vanishing from view,
Like lessening pebble it withdrew;
Still less and less, a speck of white
That gemm'd the tide, then mock'd the sight;
And all its hidden secrets sleep,
Known but to Genii of the deep,
Which, trembling in their coral caves,
They dare not whisper to the waves.

VAMPIRES IN LITERATURE

As rising on its purple wing
The insect-queen of eastern spring,
O'er emerald meadows of Kashmeer
Invites the young pursuer near,
And leads him on from flower to flower
A weary chace and wasted hour,
Then leaves him, as it soars on high
With panting heart and tearful eye:
So Beauty lures the full-grown child
With hue as bright, and wing as wild;
A chase of idle hopes and fears,
Begun in folly, closed in tears.
If won, to equal ills betrayed,
Woe waits the insect and the maid,
A life of pain, the loss of peace,
From infant's play, and man's caprice:
The lovely toy so fiercely sought
Has lost its charm by being caught,
For every touch that wooed its stay
Has brush'd its brightest hues away,
Till charm, and hue, and beauty gone,
'Tis left to fly or fall alone.
With wounded wing, or bleeding breast,
Ah! where shall either victim rest?
Can this with faded pinion soar
From rose to tulip as before?
Or Beauty, blighted in an hour,
Find joy within her broken bower?
No: gayer insects fluttering by
Ne'er droop the wing o'er those that die,
And lovelier things have mercy shewn
To every failing but their own,
And every woe a tear can claim

Except an erring sister's shame.

The Mind, that broods o'er guilty woes,
Is like the Scorpion girt by fire,
In circle narrowing as it glows
The flames around their captive close,
Till inly search'd by thousand throes,
And maddening in her ire,
One sad and sole relief she knows,
The sting she nourish'd for her foes,
Whose venom never yet was vain,
Gives but one pang, and cures all pain,
And darts into her desperate brain.—
So do the dark in soul expire,
Or live like Scorpion girt by fire
So writhes the mind by conscience riven,
Unfit for earth, undoom'd for heaven,
Darkness above, despair beneath,
Around it flame, within it death!—

Black Hassan from the haram flies,
Nor bends on woman's face his eyes,
The unwonted chace each hour employs,
Yet shares he not the hunter's joys.
Not thus was Hassan wont to fly
When Leila dwelt in his Serai.
Doth Leila there no longer dwell?
That tale can only Hassan tell:
Strange rumours in our city say
Upon that eve she fled away;
When Rhamazan's last sun was set,
And flashing from each minaret
Millions of lamps proclaim'd the feast

Of Bairam through the boundless East.
'Twas then she went as to the bath,
Which Hassan vainly search'd in wrath,
But she was flown her master's rage
In likeness of a Georgian page;
And far beyond the Moslem's power
Had wrong'd him with the faithless Giaour.
Somewhat of this had Hassan deem'd,
But still so fond, so fair she seem'd,
Too well he trusted to the slave

Whose treachery deserv'd a grave:
And on that eve had gone to mosque,
And thence to feast in his kiosk.
Such is the tale his Nubians tell,
Who did not watch their charge too well;
But others say, that on that night,
By pale Phingari's trembling light,
The Giaour upon his jet black steed
Was seen—but seen alone to speed
With bloody spur along the shore,
Nor maid nor page behind him bore.

Her eye's dark charm 'twere vain to tell,
But gaze on that of the Gazelle,
It will assist thy fancy well,
As large, as languishingly dark,
But Soul beam'd forth in every spark
That darted from beneath its lid,
Bright as the gem of Giamschid
Yea, Soul, and should our prophet say
That form was nought but breathing clay,
By Alla! I would answer nay;

VAMPIRES IN LITERATURE

Though on Al-Sirat's arch I stood,
Which totters o'er the fiery flood,
With Paradise within my view,
And all his Houris beckoning through.
Oh! who young Leila's glance could read
And keep that portion of his creed
Which saith, that woman is but dust,
A soulless toy for tyrant's lust?
On her might Muftis gaze, and own
That through her eye the Immortal shone—
On her fair cheek's unfading hue,
The young pomegranate's blossoms strew
Their bloom in blushes ever new—

Her hair in hyacinthine flow
When left to roll its folds below;
As midst her handmaids in the hall
She stood superior to them all,
Hath swept the marble where her feet
Gleamed whiter than the mountain sleet
Ere from the cloud that gave it birth,
It fell, and caught one stain of earth.

Stern Hassan hath a journey ta'en
With twenty vassals in his train,
Each arm'd as best becomes a man
With arquebuss and ataghan;
The chief before, as deck'd for war,
Bears in his belt the scimitar
Stain'd with the best of Arnaut blood,
When in the pass the rebels stood,
And few return'd to tell the tale
Of what befell in Parne's vale.

The pistols which his girdle bore
Were those that once a pasha wore,
Which still, though gemm'd and boss'd with gold,
Even robbers tremble to behold.—
'Tis said he goes to woo a bride
More true than her who left his side;
The faithless slave that broke her bower,
And, worse than faithless, for a Giaour!—

The sun's last rays are on the hill,
And sparkle in the fountain rill,
Whose welcome waters cool and clear,
Draw blessings from the mountaineer;
Here may the loitering merchant Greek
Find that repose 'twere vain to seek
In cities lodg'd too near his lord,
And trembling for his secret hoard—
Here may he rest where none can see,
In crowds a slave, in deserts free;
And with forbidden wine may stain
The bowl a Moslem must not drain.—

The foremost Tartar's in the gap,
Conspicuous by his yellow cap,
The rest in lengthening line the while
Wind slowly through the long defile;
Above, the mountain rears a peak,
Where vultures whet the thirsty beak,
And their's may be a feast to-night,
Shall tempt them down ere morrow's light.
Beneath, a river's wintry stream
Has shrunk before the summer beam,
And left a channel bleak and bare,

Save shrubs that spring to perish there.
Each side the midway path there lay
Small broken crags of granite gray,
By time or mountain lightning riven,
From summits clad in mists of heaven;
For where is he that hath beheld
The peak of Liakura unveil'd?

They reach the grove of pine at last,
"Bismillah! now the peril's past;
"For yonder view the opening plain,
"And there we'll prick our steeds amain:"
The Chiaus spake, and as he said,
A bullet whistled o'er his head;
The foremost Tartar bites the ground!
Scarce had they time to check the rein
Swift from their steeds the riders bound,
But three shall never mount again,
Unseen the foes that gave the wound,
The dying ask revenge in vain.
With steel unsheath'd, and carbines bent,
Some o'er their courser's harness leant,
Half shelter'd by the steed,
Some fly behind the nearest rock,
And there await the coming shock,
Nor tamely stand to bleed
Beneath the shaft of foes unseen,
Who dare not quit their craggy screen.
Stern Hassan only from his horse
Disdains to light, and keeps his course,
Till fiery flashes in the van
Proclaim too sure the robber-clan
Have well secur'd the only way

Could now avail the promis'd prey;
Then curl'd his very beard with ire,
And glared his eye with fiercer fire.
"Though far and near the bullets hiss,
"I've scaped a bloodier hour than this."
And now the foe their covert quit,
And call his vassals to submit;
But Hassan's frown and furious word
Are dreaded more than hostile sword,
Nor of his little band a man
Resign'd carbine or ataghan.
In fuller sight, more near and near,
The lately ambush'd foes appear,
And issuing from the grove advance,
Some who on battle charger prance.—
Who leads them on with foreign brand,
Far flashing in his red right hand?
"'Tis he—'tis he—I know him now,
"I know him by his pallid brow;
"I know him by the evil eye
"That aids bis envious treachery;
"I know him by his jet-black barb,
"Though now array'd in Arnaut garb,
"Apostate from his own vile faith,
"It shall not save him from the death;
"'Tis he, well met in any hour,
"Lost Leila's love—accursed Giaour!"

With sabre shiver'd to the hilt,
Yet dripping with the blood he spilt;
Yet strain'd within the sever'd hand
That quivers round the faithless brand;
His turban far behind him roll'd,

And cleft in twain its firmest fold;
His flowing robe by falchion torn,
And crimson as those clouds of morn
That streak'd with dusky red, portend
The day shall have a stormy end;
A stain on every bush that bore
A fragment of his palampore
His heart with wounds unnumber'd riven,
His back to earth, his face to heaven,
Fall'n Hassan lies—his unclos'd eye
Yet lowering on his enemy,
As if the hour that seal'd his fate,
Surviving left bis quenchless hate;
And o'er him bends that foe with brow
As dark as his that bled below.—

"Yes, Leila sleeps beneath the wave,
"But his shall be a redder grave;
"Her spirit pointed well the steel
"Which taught that felon heart to feel.
"He call'd the Prophet, but his power
"Was vain against the vengeful Giaour:
"He call'd on Alla—but the word
"Arose unheeded or unheard.
"Thou Paynim fool!—could Leila's prayer
"Be pass'd, and thine accorded there?
"I watch'd my time, I leagu'd with these,
"The traitor in his turn to seize;
"My wrath is wreak'd, the deed is done,
"And now I go—but go alone."

A turban carv'd in coarsest stone,
A pillar with rank weeds o'ergrown,

Whereon can now be scarcely read
The Koran verse that mourns the dead;
Point out the spot where Hassan fell
A victim in that lonely dell.
There sleeps as true an Osmanlie
As e'er at Mecca bent the knee;
As ever scorn'd forbidden wine,
Or pray'd with face towards the shrine,
In orisons resumed anew
At solemn sound of "Alla Hu!"
Yet died he by a stranger's hand,
And stranger in his native land—
Yet died he as in arms he stood,
And unaveng'd, at least in blood.
But him the maids of Paradise
Impatient to their halls invite,
And the dark Heaven of Houri's eyes
On him shall glance for ever bright;
They come—their kerchiefs green they wave,
And welcome with a kiss the brave!
Who falls in battle 'gainst a Giaour,
Is worthiest an immortal bower.

But thou, false Infidel! shalt writhe
Beneath avenging Monkir's scythe;
And from its torment 'scape alone
To wauder round lost Eblis' throne;
And fire unquench'd, unquenchable—
Around—within—thy heart shall dwell,
Nor ear can hear, nor tongue can tell
The tortures of that inward hell!—
But first, on earth as Vampire sent,
Thy corse shall from its tomb be rent;

Then ghastly haunt thy native place,
And suck the blood of all thy race,
There from thy daughter, sister, wife,
At midnight drain the stream of life;
Yet loathe the banquet which perforce
Must feed thy livid living corse;
Thy victims ere they yet expire
Shall know the dæmon for their sire,
As cursing thee, thou cursing them,
Thy flowers are wither'd on the stem.
But one that for thy crime must fall—
The youngest—most belov'd of all,
Shall bless thee with a father's name—
That word shall wrap thy heart in flame!
Yet must thou end thy task, and mark
Her cheek's last tinge, her eye's last spark,
And the last glassy glance must view
Which freezes o'er its lifeless blue;
Then with unhallowed hand shalt tear
The tresses of her yellow hair,
Of which in life a lock when shorn,
Affection's fondest pledge was worn;
But now is borne away by thee,
Memorial of thine agony!

Wet with thine own best blood shall drip,
Thy gnashing tooth and haggard lip;
Then stalking to thy sullen grave—
Go—and with Gouls and Afrits rave;
Till these in horror shrink away
From spectre more accursed than they!

"How name ye yon lone Caloyer?

"His features I have scann'd before
"In mine own land—'tis many a year,
"Since, dashing by the lonely shore,
"I saw him urge as fleet a steed
"As ever serv'd a horseman's need.
"But once I saw that face—but then
"It was so mark'd with inward pain
"I could not pass it by again;
"It breathes the same dark spirit now,
"As death were stamped upon his brow.

"'Tis twice three years at summer tide
"Since first among our freres he came;
"And here it soothes him to abide
"For some dark deed he will not name.
"But never at our vesper prayer,
"Nor e'er before confession chair
"Kneels he, nor recks he when arise
"Incense or anthem to the skies,
"But broods within his cell alone,
"His faith and race alike unknown.
"The sea from Paynim land he crost,
"And here ascended from the coast,
"Yet seems he not of Othman race,
"But only Christian in his face:
"I'd judge him some stray renegade,
"Repentant of the change he made,

"Save that he shuns our holy shrine,
"Nor tastes the sacred bread and wine.
"Great largess to these walls he brought,
"And thus our abbot's favour bought;
"But were I Prior, not a day

"Should brook such stranger's further stay,
"Or pent within our penance cell
"Should doom him there for aye to dwell.
"Much in his visions mutters he
"Of maiden 'whelmed beneath the sea;
"Of sabres clashing—foemen flying,
"Wrongs aveng'd—and Moslem dying.
"On cliff he hath been known to stand,
"And rave as to some bloody hand
"Fresh sever'd from its parent limb,
"Invisible to all but him,
"Which beckons onward to his grave,
"And lures to leap into the wave."

To love the softest hearts are prone,
But such can ne'er be all his own;
Too timid in his woes to share,
Too meek to meet, or brave despair;
And sterner hearts alone may feel
The wound that time can never heal.
The rugged metal of the mine
Must burn before its surface shine,
But plung'd within the furnace-flame,
It bends and melts—though still the same;
Then tempered to thy want, or will,
'Twill serve thee to defend or kill;
A breast-plate for thine hour of need,
Or blade to bid thy foeman bleed;
But if a dagger's form it bear,
Let those, who shape it's edge, beware!
Thus passion's fire, and woman's art,
Can turn and tame the sterner heart;
From these it's form and tone is ta'en,

And what they make it, must remain,
But break—before it bend again.

If solitude succeed to grief,
Release from pain is slight relief;
The vacant bosom's wilderness
Might thank the pang that made it less.
We loathe what none are left to share—
Even bliss—'twere woe alone to bear;
The heart once left thus desolate,
Must fly at last for ease—to hate.
It is as if the dead could feel
The icy worm around them steal,
And shudder, as the reptiles creep
To revel o'er their rotting sleep
Without the power to scare away
The cold consumers of their clay!
It is as if the desart-bird,
Whose beak unlocks her bosom's stream;
To still her famish'd nestlings' scream,
Nor mourns a life to them transferr'd;
Should rend her rash devoted breast,
And find them flown her empty nest.
The keenest pangs the wretched find
Are rapture to the dreary void—
The leafless desart of the mind—
The waste of feelings unemploy'd—
Who would be doom'd to gaze upon
A sky without a cloud or sun?
Less hideous far the tempest's roar,
Than ne'er to brave the billows more—
Thrown, when the war of winds is o'er,
A lonely wreck on fortune's shore,

'Mid sullen calm, and silent bay,
Unseen to drop by dull decay;—
Better to sink beneath the shock
Than moulder piecemeal on the rock!

"Father! thy days have pass'd in peace,
"'Mid counted beads, and countless prayer;
"To bid the sins of others cease,
"Thyself without a crime or care,
"Save transient ills that all must bear,
"Has been thy lot, from youth to age,
"And thou wilt bless thee from the rage
"Of passions fierce and uncontroul'd,
"Such as thy penitents unfold,
"Whose secret sins and sorrows rest
"Within thy pure and pitying breast.
"My days, though few, have pass'd below
"In much of joy, but more of woe;
"Yet still in hours of love or strife
"I've scap'd the weariness of life;
"Now leagu'd with friends, now girt by foes,
"I loath'd the languor of repose;
"Now nothing left to love or hate,
"No more with hope or pride clate;
"I'd rather be the thing that crawls
"Most noxious o'er a dungeon's walls,
"Than pass my dull, unvarying days,
"Condemn'd to meditate and gaze;
"Yet, lurks a wish within my breast
"For rest—but not to feel 'tis rest—
"Soon shall my fate that wish fulfil;'
"And I shall sleep without the dream
"Of what I was, and would be still,

"Though Hope hath long withdrawn her beam.

"I lov'd her, friar! nay, adored—
"But these are words that all can use
"I prov'd it more in deed than word—
"There's blood upon that dinted sword—
"A stain it's steel can never lose:
"'Twas shed for her, who died for me,
"It warmed the heart of one abhorred:
"Nay, start not—no—nor bend thy knee,
"Nor midst my sins such act record,
"Thou wilt absolve me from the deed,
"For he was hostile to thy creed!
"The very name of Nazarene
"Was wormwood to his Paynim spleen,
"Ungrateful fool! since but for brands,
"Well wielded in some bardy hands;
"And wounds by Galileans given,
"The surest pass to Turkish heav'n;
"For him his Houris still might wait
"Impatient at the prophet's gate.
"I lov'd her—love will find its way
"Through paths where wolves would fear to prey,
"And if it dares enough, 'twere hard
"If passion met not some reward—
"No matter how—or where—or why,
"I did not vainly seek—nor sigh:
"Yet sometimes with remorse in vain
"I wish she had not lov'd again.
"She died—I dare not tell thee how,
"But look—'tis written on my brow!
"There read of Cain the curse and crime,
"In characters unworn by time:

"Still, ere thou dost condemn me—pause—
"Not mine the act, though mine the cause;
"Yet did he but what I had done
"Had she been false to more than one;
"Faithless to him-he gave the blow,
"But true to me—I laid him low;
"Howe'er deserv'd her doom might be,
"Her treachery was truth to me;
"To me she gave her heart, that all
"Which tyranny can ne'er enthrall;
"And I, alas! too late to save,
"Yet all I then could give—I gave—
"'Twas some relief—our foe a grave.
"His death sits lightly; but her fate
"Has made me—what thou well may'st hate.
"His doom was seal'd—he knew it well,
"Warn'd by the voice of stern Taheer,
"Deep in whose darkly boding ear
"The deathshot peal'd of murder near—
"As filed the troop to where they fell!

"The cold in clime are cold in blood,
"Their love can scarce deserve the name;
"But mine was like the lava flood
"That boils in Ætna's breast of flame,
"I cannot prate in puling strains
"Of ladye-love, and beauty's chain;
"If changing cheek—and scorching vein—
"Lips taught to writhe—but not complain—
"If bursting heart, and mad'ning brain,
"And daring deed, and vengeful steel,
"And all that I have felt—and feel—
"Betoken love—that love was mine,

"And shewn by many a bitter sign.
"'Tis true, I could not whine nor sigh,
"I knew but to obtain or die.
"I die—but first I have possest,
"And come what may, I have been blest;

"Even now alone, yet undismay'd,
"(I know no friend, and ask no aid,)
"But for the thought of Leila slain,
"Give me the pleasure with the pain,
"So would I live and love again.
"I grieve, but not, my holy guide!
"For him who dies, but her who died;
"She sleeps beneath the wandering wave,
"Ah! had she but an earthly grave,
"This breaking heart and throbbing head
"Should seek and share her narrow bed.

"Tell me no more of fancy's gleam,
"No, father, no, 'twas not a dream;
"Alas! the dreamer first must sleep,
"I only watch'd, and wish'd to weep;
"But could not, for my burning brow
"Throbb'd to the very brain as now.
"I wish'd but for a single tear,
"As something welcome, new, and dear;
"I wish'd it then—I wish it still,
"Despair is stronger than my will.
"Waste not thine orison—despair
"Is mightier than thy pious prayer;
"I would not, if I might, be blest,
"I want no paradise—but rest.
"'Twas then, I tell thee, father! then

"I saw her—yes—she liv'd again;
"And shining in her white symar,
"As through yon pale grey cloud—the star
"Which now I gaze on, as on her
"Who look'd and looks far lovelier;
"Dimly I view its trembling spark—
"To-morrow's night shall be more dark—
"And I—before its rays appear,
"That lifeless thing the living fear.
"I wander, father! for my soul
"Is fleeting towards the final goal;
"I saw her, friar! and I rose,
"Forgetful of our former woes;
"And rushing from my couch, I dart,
"And clasp her to my desperate heart;
"I clasp—what is it that I clasp?
"No breathing form within my grasp,
"No heart that beats reply to mine,
"Yet, Leila! yet the form is thine!
"And art thou, dearest, chang'd so much,
"As meet my eye, yet mock my touch?
"Ah! were thy beauties e'er so cold,
"I care not—so my arms enfold
"The all they ever wish'd to hold.
"Alas! around a shadow prest,
"They shrink upon my lonely breast;
"Yet still—'tis there—in silence stands,
"And beckons with beseeching hands!
"With braided hair, and bright-black eye—
"I kuew 'twas false—she could not die!
"But he is dead—within the dell
"I saw him buried where he fell;
"He comes not—for he cannot break

"From earth—why then art thou awake?
"They told me, wild waves roll'd above
"The face I view, the form I love;
"They told me—'twas a hideous tale!
"I'd tell it—but my tongue would fail—
"If true—and from thine ocean-cave
"Thou com'st to claim a calmer grave;
"Oh! pass thy dewy fingers o'er
"This brow that then will burn no more;
"Or place them on my hopeless heart—
"But, shape or shade!—whate'er thou art,
"In mercy, ne'er again depart—
"Or farther with thee bear my soul,
"Than winds can waft—or waters roll!—

"Such is my name, and such my tale,
"Confessor to thy secret ear,
"I breathe the sorrows I bewail,
"And thank thee for the generous tear
"This glazing eye could never shed,
"Then lay me with the humblest dead,
"And save the cross above my head;
"Be neither name nor emblem laid
"By prying stranger to be read,
"Or stay the passing pilgrim's tread."
He pass'd—nor of his name and race
Hath left a token or a trace,
Save what the father must not say
Who shrived him on his dying day;
This broken tale was all we knew
Of her he lov'd, or him he slew.

Der Vampire
Heinrich August Ossenfelder

My dear young maiden clingeth
Unbending fast and firm
To all the long-held teaching
Of a mother ever true;
As in vampires unmortal
Folk on the Theyse's portal
Heyduck-like do believe.
But my Christine thou dost dally,
And wilt my loving parry
Till I myself avenging
To a vampire's health a-drinking
Him toast in pale tockay.

And as softly thou art sleeping
To thee shall I come creeping
And thy life's blood drain away.
And so shalt thou be trembling
For thus shall I be kissing
And death's threshold thou' it be crossing
With fear, in my cold arms.
And last shall I thee question
Compared to such instruction
What are a mother's charms?

(Translated from original German by Unknown)

The Bride of Corinth
Johann Wolfgang von Goethe

ONCE a stranger youth to Corinth came,
Who in Athens lived, but hoped that he
From a certain townsman there might claim,
As his father's friend, kind courtesy.
Son and daughter, they
Had been wont to say
Should thereafter bride and bridegroom be.

But can he that boon so highly prized,
Save tis dearly bought, now hope to get?
They are Christians and have been baptized,
He and all of his are heathens yet.
For a newborn creed,
Like some loathsome weed,
Love and truth to root out oft will threat.

Father, daughter, all had gone to rest,
And the mother only watches late;
She receives with courtesy the guest,
And conducts him to the room of state.
Wine and food are brought,
Ere by him besought

Bidding him good night she leaves him straight.

But he feels no relish now, in truth,
For the dainties so profusely spread;
Meat and drink forgets the wearied youth,
And, still dress'd, he lays him on the bed.
Scarce are closed his eyes,
When a form in-hies
Through the open door with silent tread.

By his glimmering lamp discerns he now
How, in veil and garment white array'd,
With a black and gold band round her brow,
Glides into the room a bashful maid.
But she, at his sight,
Lifts her hand so white,
And appears as though full sore afraid.

"Am I," cries she, "such a stranger here,
That the guest's approach they could not name?
Ah, they keep me in my cloister drear,
Well nigh feel I vanquish'd by my shame.
On thy soft couch now
Slumber calmly thou!
"I'll return as swiftly as I came."

"Stay, thou fairest maiden!" cries the boy,
Starting from his couch with eager haste:
"Here are Ceres', Bacchus' gifts of joy;
Amor bringest thou, with beauty grac'd!
Thou art pale with fear!
Loved one let us here
Prove the raptures the Immortals taste."

"Draw not nigh, O Youth! afar remain!
Rapture now can never smile on me;
For the fatal step, alas! is ta'en,
Through my mother's sick-bed phantasy.
Cured, she made this oath:
'Youth and nature both
Shall henceforth to Heav'n devoted be.'

From the house, so silent now, are driven

All the gods who reign'd supreme of yore;
One Invisible now rules in heaven,
On the cross a Saviour they adore.
Victims slay they here,
Neither lamb nor steer,
But the altars reek with human gore.

And he lists, and ev'ry word he weighs,
While his eager soul drinks in each sound:
"Can it be that now before my gaze
Stands my loved one on this silent ground? Pledge to me
thy troth!
Through our father's oath:
With Heav'ns blessing will our love be crown'd."

"Kindly youth, I never can be thine!
'Tis my sister they intend for thee.
When I in the silent cloister pine,
Ah, within her arms remember me!
Thee alone I love,
While love's pangs I prove
Soon the earth will veil my misery."

"No! for by this glowing flame I swear,
Hymen hath himself propitious shown:
Let us to my fathers house repair,
And thoult find that joy is not yet flown,
Sweetest, here then stay,
And without delay
Hold we now our wedding feast alone!"

Then exchange they tokens of their truth;
She gives him a golden chain to wear,

And a silver chalice would the youth
Give her in return of beauty rare.
"That is not for me;
Yet I beg of thee,
One lock only give me of thy hair."

Now the ghostly hour of midnight knell'd,
And she seem'd right joyous at the sign;
To her pallid lips the cup she held,
But she drank of nought but blood-red wine.
For to taste the bread
There before them spread,
Nought he spoke could make the maid incline.

To the youth the goblet then she brought,—
He too quaff'd with eager joy the bowl.
Love to crown the silent feast he sought,
Ah! full love-sick was the stripling's soul.
From his prayer she shrinks,
Till at length he sinks
On the bed and weeps without control.

And she comes, and lays her near the boy:
"How I grieve to see thee sorrowing so!
If thou think'st to clasp my form with joy,
Thou must learn this secret sad to know;
Yes! the maid, whom thou
Call'st thy loved one now,
Is as cold as ice, though white as snow."

Then he clasps her madly in his arm,
While love's youthful might pervades his frame:
"Thou might'st hope, when with me, to grow warm.

E'en if from the grave thy spirit came!
Breath for breath, and kiss!
Overflow of bliss!
Dost not thou, like me, feel passion's flame?"

Love still closer rivets now their lips,
Tears they mingle with their rapture blest,
From his mouth the flame she wildly sips,
Each is with the other's thought possess'd.
His hot ardour's flood
Warms her chilly blood,
But no heart is beating in her breast.

In her care to see that nought went wrong,
Now the mother happen'd to draw near;
t the door long hearkens she, full long,
Wond'ring at the sounds that greet her ear.
Tones of joy and sadness,
And love's blissful madness,
As of bride and bridegroom they appear.

From the door she will not now remove
'Till she gains full certainty of this;
And with anger hears she vows of love,
Soft caressing words of mutual bliss.
"Hush! the cock's loud strain!
But thoult come again,
When the night returns!"–then kiss on kiss.

Then her wrath the mother cannot hold,
But unfastens straight the lock with ease
"In this house are girls become so bold,
As to seek e'en strangers' lusts to please?"

By her lamp's clear glow
Looks she in,–and oh!
Sight of horror!–'tis her child she sees.

Fain the youth would, in his first alarm,
With the veil that o'er her had been spread,
With the carpet, shield his love from harm;
But she casts them from her, void of dread,
And with spirit's strength,
In its spectre length,
Lifts her figure slowly from the bed.

"Mother! mother!"–Thus her wan lips say:
"May not I one night of rapture share?
From the warm couch am I chased away?
Do I waken only to despair?
It contents not thee
To have driven me
An untimely shroud of death to wear?

"But from out my coffin's prison-bounds
By a wond'rous fate I'm forced to rove,
While the blessings and the chaunting sounds
That your priests delight in, useless prove.
Water, salt, are vain
Fervent youth to chain,
Ah, e'en Earth can never cool down love!

"When that infant vow of love was spoken,
Venus' radiant temple smiled on both.
Mother! thou that promise since hast broken,
Fetter'd by a strange, deceitful oath.
Gods, though, hearken ne'er,

VAMPIRES IN LITERATURE

Should a mother swear
To deny her daughter's plighted troth.

From my grave to wander I am forc'd,
Still to seek The Good's long-sever'd link,
Still to love the bridegroom I have lost,
And the life-blood of his heart to drink;
When his race is run,
I must hasten on,
And the young must 'neath my vengeance sink.

"Beauteous youth! no longer mayst thou live;
Here must shrivel up thy form so fair;
Did not I to thee a token give,
Taking in return this lock of hair?
View it to thy sorrow!
Grey thoult be to-morrow,
Only to grow brown again when there.

"Mother, to this final prayer give ear!
Let a funeral pile be straightway dress'd;
Open then my cell so sad and drear,
That the flames may give the lovers rest!
When ascends the fire
From the glowing pyre,
To the gods of old we'll hasten, blest."

(English Translation by Unknown)
[See, "Bride of Corinth Based On" in back of book for
further information.]

The Vampire
Charles Baudelaire

VAMPIRES IN LITERATURE

Thou who abruptly as a knife
Didst come into my heart; thou who,
A demon horde into my life,
Didst enter, wildly dancing, through

The doorways of my sense unlatched
To make my spirit thy domain —
Harlot to whom I am attached
As convicts to the ball and chain,

As gamblers to the wheel's bright spell,
As drunkards to their raging thirst,
As corpses to their worms — accurst
Be thou! Oh, be thou damned to hell!

I have entreated the swift sword
To strike, that I at once be freed;
The poisoned phial I have implored
To plot with me a ruthless deed.

Alas! the phial and the blade
Do cry aloud and laugh at me:
"Thou art not worthy of our aid;
Thou art not worthy to be free.

"Though one of us should be the tool
To save thee from thy wretched fate,
Thy kisses would resuscitate
The body of thy vampire, fool!"

(Translated from the French by George Dillon; Flowers of
Evil (NY: Harper and Brothers, 1936))

The Vampyre
James Clerk Maxwell

There is a knight riding through the wood
And a doughty knight is he
And surely he delivering a message
He rides so hastily

He passes the Oak and he passes the Birch
And he passes many a tree
But pleasant to him was the tree so slim
For beneath it he did see

The bonniest lady that ever he saw
She was so shining and fair ...
... But her rosy cheek grew ghostly pale
And she seemed as she was dead

And the false, false knight grew pale with fright
And his hair rose up on end.
For bygone days came to his mind
And he recognized his former love

Then the lady spoke—"Thou, false knight,
Have done me much ill
Thou didst forsake me long ago
But I am constant still.

For, though I lie in the woods so cold
I cannot be at rest
Until I suck the good life blood
Of the man who made me die."

He saw her lips were wet with blood

And he saw her lifeless eyes
And loud he cried, "Get from my side,
Thou vampire corpse unclean!"

But, no, he is in her magic boat
And on that wide, wide sea.
And the vampire sucks his good life's blood
She sucks him until he dies.

So, now, beware, whoever you are
That walks in this lone wood
Beware of that deceitful sprite
The ghost that suckles the blood.

(Publisher's Note: The above poem was written in Scottish
by James Clerk Maxwell in 1845 when he was 15.
Translation by Unknown.)

The Vampyre
Owen Meredith (Lord Lytton)

VAMPIRES IN LITERATURE

I found a corpse, with golden hair,
Of a maiden seven months dead.
But the face, with the death in it, still was fair,
And the lips with their love were red.
Rose leaves on a snow-drift shed,
Blood-drops by Adonis bled,
Doubtless were not so red.

I combed her hair into curls of gold,
And I kissed her lips till her lips were warm,
And I bathed her body in moonlight cold,
'Till she grew to a living form:
Till she stood up bold to a magic of old,
And walked to a muttered charm –
Lifelike, without alarm.

And she walks by me, and she talks by me,
Evermore, night and day;
For she loves me so, that, wherever I go,
She follows me all the way –
This corpse – you would almost say
There pined a soul in the clay.

Her eyes are so bright at the dead of night
That they keep me wake with dread:
And my life-blood fails in my veins, and pales
At the sight of her lips so red:
For her face is as white as the pillow by night
Where she kisses me on my bed:
All her gold hair outspread –
Neither alive nor dead.

VAMPIRES IN LITERATURE

I would that this woman's head
Were less golden about the hair:
I would her lips were less red,
And her face less deadly fair.
For this is the worst to bear –
How came that redness there?

'Tis my heart, be sure, she eats for her food;
And it makes one's whole flesh creep
To think that she drinks and drains my blood
Unawares, when I am asleep.
How could those red lips
Their redness so damson-deep?

There's a thought like a serpent, slips
Ever into my heart and head, —
There are plenty of women, alive and human
One might woo, if one wished, and wed –
Women with hearts, and brains, — ay – and lips
Not so terribly red.

But to house with a corpse – and she so fair,
With that dim, unearthly, golden hair,
And those sad, serene, blue eyes,
With their looks from who knows where,
Which death has made so wise,
With the grave's own secret there –
It is more than I can bear!

It were better for me, ere I cam nigh her,
This corpse – ere I looked upon her,
Had they burned my body in flame and fire
With a sorcerer's dishonor.

For when the Devil hath made his lair,
And lurks in the eyes of a fair young woman
(To grieve a man's soul with her golden hair,
And break his heart, if his heart be human),
Would not a saint despair
To be saved by fast or prayer
From perdition made so fair?

The Vampire
Delmira Agustini

147

VAMPIRES IN LITERATURE

In the bosom of the sad evening
I called upon your sorrow... Feeling it was
Feeling your heart as well. You were pale
Even your voice, your waxen eyelids,

Lowered... and remained silent... You seemed
To hear death passing by... I who had opened
Your wound bit on it—did you feel me?—
As into the gold of a honeycomb I bit!

I squeezed even more treacherously, sweetly
Your heart mortally wounded,
By the cruel dagger, rare and exquisite,
Of a nameless illness, until making it bleed in sobs!
And the thousand mouths of my damned thirst
I offered to that open fountain in your suffering.

Why was I your vampire of bitterness?
Am I a flower or a breed of an obscure species
That devours sores and gulps tears?

Strigoiul (Vampyre)

Vasile Alecsandri

VAMPIRES IN LITERATURE

Near the cliff's sharp edge, on high
Standing out against the sky,
Dost thou see a ruined cross
Weatherstained, o'ergrown by moss,
Gloomy, desolate, forsaken,
By unnumbered tempests shaken?

Not a blade of grass grows nigh it,
Not a peasant lingers by it.
E'en the sombre bird of night
Shuns it in her darksome flight,
Startled by the piteous groan
That arises from the stone.

All around, on starless nights,
Myriad hosts of livid lights
Flicker fretfully, revealing
At its foot a phantom, kneeling
Whilst it jabbers dismal plaints,
Cursing God and all the saints.

Tardy traveller, beware
Of that spectre gibbering there;
Close your eyes, and urge your steed
To the utmost of his speed;–
For beneath that cross, I ween,
Lies a Vampyre's corpse obscene!

Though the night is black and cold
Love's found story, often told,
Floats in whispers through the air,

VAMPIRES IN LITERATURE

Stalwart youth and maiden fair
Seal sweet vows of ardent passion
With their lips, in lovers' fashion.

"Restless, pale, a shape I see
Hov'ring nigh; what may it be?
'Tis a charger, white as snow,
Pacing slowly to and fro
Like a sentry. As he turns
Haughtily the sward he spurns.

"Leave me not, beloved, tonight!
Stay with me till morning's light!'
Weeping, thus besought the maid;
'Love, my soul is sore afraid!
Brave not the dread Vampyre's power,
Mightiest at this mystic hour!'

Not a word he spake, but prest
The sobbing maiden to his breast;
Kissed her lips and cheeks and eyes
Heedless of her tears and sighs;
Waved his hand, with gesture gay,
Mounted–smiled–and rode away.

We rides across the dusky plain
Tearing along with might and main
Like some wild storm-fiend, in his flight
Nursed on the ebony breast of Night?
'Tis he, who left her in her need–
Her lover, on his milk-white steed!

The blast in all its savage force
Strives to o'erthrow the gallant horse
That snorts defiance to his foe
And struggles onward. See! below
The causeway, 'long the river-side
A thousand flutt'ring flamelets glide!

Now they approach, and now recede,
  Still followed by the panting steed;
He nears the ruined cross! A crash,
  A piteous cry, a heavy splash,
    And in the rocky river-bed
Rider and horse lie crushed and dead.
Then from those dismal depths arise
Blaspheming yells and strident cries
Re-echoing through the murky air
And, like a serpent from its lair,
Brandishing high a blood-stained glaive
The Vampyre rises from his grave!

(Translated by William B. Kingston)

The Vampire
Arthur Symons

Intolerable woman, where's the name
For your insane complexity of shame?
Vampire! white bloodless creature of the night,
Whose lust of blood has blanched her chill veins white,
Veins fed with moonlight over dead men's tombs;
Whose eyes remember many martyrdoms.

So that their depths, whose depth cannot be found.
Are shadowed pools in which a soul lies drowned;
Who would fain have pity, but she may not rest
Till she have sucked a man's heart from his breast,
And drained his life-blood from him, vein by vein,
And seen his eyes grow brighter for the pain,
And his lips sigh her name with his last breath.
As the man swoons ecstatically on death.

The Vampyre
James Clerk Maxwell

Thair is a knichte rydis through the wood,
And a doughty knichte is tree,
And sure hee is on a message sent,
He rydis see hastilie.

Hee passit the aik, and hee passit the birk,
And hee passit monie a tre,
Bot plesant to him was the saugh sae slim,
For beneath it hee did see
The boniest ladye that ever he saw,
Scho was see schyn and fair.
And there scho sat, beneath the saugh,
Kaiming hir gowden hair.

And then the knichte—"Oh ladye brichte,
What chance hes brought you here,
But say the word, and ye schall gang
Back to your kindred dear."
Then up and spok the Ladye fair—
"I have nae friends or kin,
Bot in a littel boat I live,
Amidst the waves' loud din."

Then answered thus the douchty knichte—
"I'll follow you through all,
For gin ye bee in a littel boat,
The world to it seemis small."
They gaed through the wood, and through the wood
To the end of the wood they came:
And when they came to the end of the wood
They saw the salt sea faem.

And then they saw the wee, wee boat,
That daunced on the top of the wave,
And first got in the ladye fair,
And then the knichte sae brave;
They got into the wee, wee boat,
And rowed wi' a' their micht;
When the knichte sae brave, he turnit about,
And lookit at the ladye bricht;
He lookit at her bonie cheik,
And hee lookit at hir twa bricht eyne,
Bot hir rosie cheik growe ghaistly pale,
And scho seymit as scho deid had been.

The fause fause knichte growe pale wi frichte,
And his hair rose up on end,
For gane-by days cam to his mynde,
And his former luve he kenned.
Then spake the ladye,—"Thou, fause knichte,
Hast done to mee much ill,
Thou didst forsake me long ago,
Bot I am constant still;
For though I ligg in the woods sae cald,
At rest I canna bee
Until I sucke the gude lyfe blude
Of the man that gart me dee."

Hee saw hir lipps were wet wi' blude,
And hee saw hir lyfelesse eyne,
And loud hee cry'd, "Get frae my syde,
Thou vampyr corps uncleane!"

Bot no, hee is in hir magic boat,
And on the wyde wyde sea;
And the vampyr suckis his gude lyfe blude,
Sho suckis hym till hee dee.

So now beware, whoe're you are,
That walkis in this lone wood;
Beware of that deceitfull spright,
The ghaist that suckle the blude.

The Vampyres
Mihai Eminescu

I

... for it fades away like smoke above the earth.
They bloomed like flowers, were cut like grass,
Wrapped up in a linen and buried in the ground

Within an ancient church with lofty soaring dome,
Between tall waxen candles, does in her coffin lie,
Her face towards the altar, wrapped in white drapery,
The bride of brave King Harold, the King of Avari,
While softly chanted dirges do from the darkness come.

Upon the dead girl's breast a wreath of jewels glows,
Her golden hair hangs loosely over the coffin side,
Her eyes are sunken deep; a sad smile sanctified
Rest on her parched lips, that death to mauve has dyed,
While is her lovely face as pale as winter snows.

Beside her on his knees is Harold, mighty King,
And from his bloodshot eyes does shine untold despair,
His mouth with pain is drawn, dishevelled is his hair.
Though like a lion he would roar, grief holds him si-
lent there;
Three days he thinks upon his life in nameless sorrowing.

"I was still but a child. Within the pine-tree glade
My greedy eyes already had conquered many a land,
I dreamed an empire grow beneath my fancy's wand,
I dreamed the world entire was under my command,
The foaming Volga's ford I fathomed with my blade.

VAMPIRES IN LITERATURE

Countless mighty hosts my youthful zeal led forth
By whom as of some God my name was worshipped.
I felt the very earth tremble beneath my tread;
Before my marching hosts the wandering nations fled,
Crowding in their terror the empty frozen North.

For Odin had deserted his frosty ancient home,
Down long and tortuous ways his wandering people went;
Priests with snowy locks and backs that time had bent
Roused and led through forests where peace an age
had spent
Thousand diverse tongues along the way to Rome.

One eve my troops I camped upon the Nistru's side,
Intending on the morrow your battle host to quell;
But there amidst your councillors I came beneath your spell;
Before your marble loveliness my eyes in wonder fell,
So fearless you stood, in all your childish pride.

Before your soft reproach my words dried on my tongue.
I strove to make an answer, but could no answer find.
Would earth have swallowed me, and left no trace behind,
My hands before my face I put my shame to blind,
And tears came to the eyes where tears had never sprung.

Your councillors did smile and soon departed then
To leave us quite alone. I asked you, after a space,
Though scarcely did I dare to look upon your face;
Why have you come, o Queen, into this desert place?
What do you seek so far away from courts and men?

In a murmur filled with tears, gentle and sad you spake
Holding me with your eyes in which the sky shone clear,
You said: "I beg of you, o King and cavalier,
To give to me as prisoner the one I hold most dear,
Harold, that untamed youth, him would I captive take."

Turning my head away, I handed you my sword.
My people ceased their march along the Danube side;
Harold no longer dreamed the universe to ride,
His ears for tender tones and poetry did abide,
The conqueror from that hour was vanquished by
your word.

From then sweet maid with hair of gold as ripened grain
Each night you came to me when nobody should know,
And your white, slender arms around my neck did throw,
And raising coaxing lips to mine you said in whispers low:
"O, King, it is for Harold I come to beg again."

If you would ask for Rome, if you would ask the earth,
Or all the crowns that rest on mortal monarch's head,
The wandering stars that beam across the heavens shed,
There heaped about your feet would I bestow instead,
But do not ask for Harold for he is nothing worth.

Ah, where are gone the days when brave I probed the ford
To stride into the world. Far better had it been
If so much loveliness my eyes had never seen...
To ride through ruined towns, to lead the battle keen
And thus fulfil those dreams the pine-tree forest stored I"

The torches are raised up. The train moves slowly on.
The Danube Queen is carried down to her narrow bed,
Councillor and monarch with heavy drooping head,
Priests with snowy beards and eyes that tears shed,
Mumbling their dirge in mournful unison.

Beneath the arching vault the slow procession goes,
A mystery religion, a strange and sombre lore,
They lower down the coffin beneath the gaping floor,
Then close it with a cross, a seal for evermore,
Beneath the holy lamp that in the corner glows.

II

Be silent, in God's name,
To hear the bay
Of the earth-hound
Under the stone cross.

Harold on his charger sweeps far o'er hill and dale,
Like a dream he goes within the moon's pale zone;
Across his breast in folds his black cloak he has thrown,
Behind him drifts of leaves high in the air are blown,
While never straight before him the Polar Star does sail.

Reaching at last the forest that clothes the rising hills,
Where does a sweet spring murmur, well out from 'neath
a stone,
Where grey with scattered ashes an old hearth stands alone,
Where far off in the forest the earth-hound sounds his tone
And with his distant barking he midnight silence fills.

Upon a rocky ledge, quite stiff and ashen faced,
There sits, with crutch in hand, a priest of pagan creed
For ages sits he thus, by death forgot indeed,
Moss growing on his forehead and on his breast long weed,
His beard reaching to the ground, his eyebrows to his waist.;

Blindly thus for ages he sits both day and night,
Until his feet have grown one with the stone at last,
Numbering the days that numberless have passed,
While over him are circling in endless circles vast
Two crows on weary wings, one black, the other white.

And now upon his arm the youth doth sudden lay
His eager hand, and wakes the old priest terrified;
"To you, o timeless Seer, across the world I ride
To give me back the one that envious death does hide,
And all my days for you I will unceasing pray."

Now with his crutch the Seer his heavy eyebrows parts
And gazes on the King, but not an utterance makes.
Then out o'the stone's grey substance his feet with trouble
And turning towards the forest his battered crutch he
shakes,
And lastly up the narrow path with heavy paces starts.

Upon the oaken doorway that guards the mountain keep
With crutch on high uplifted loud three times does
he knock;
With thunderous commotion the gates slow back-
wards rock,
The priest kneels down... while through the young king's
spirit flock
A thousand dreadful fears, and thousand terrors leap.

Into the lofty vault of shining marble black
They go. The door swings shut again with rumbling sound;
The Seer now lights a candle that spreads its glow around
And throws away behind them their shadows on the ground
And lights the sombre walls that shine like iron back.

There in the dreadful darkness they know not what will
come...

The old magician makes a sign that he should bide,
And Harold crouches down, his sword clasped at his side,
While nameless, awful dread does through his spirit ride,
Blank gazing at the walls of that uncanny tomb.

Till soon the Seer did seem immeasurably to grow;
He waved kiss magic crutch above his ancient head,
And through the chilly vault a wind in wailing sped
And thousand whispering voices into the silence shed
A song the filled the dome with gentle cadence low.

And now the singing gradually increases like a breeze
Until with sudden swelling it to a tempest grows,
As though a gale that madly across the ocean blows,
As though the tortured soul of deepest earth arose
And all that lives and feels with horrid fright must freeze.

The mighty vault now trembles from ceiling to the floor,
The marble walls are rocking and crack right to their base
While through the darkness curses do sobs in panic chase,
And cries and moans and lightning amidst the tumult race
Till thunderous indeed has grown the wild uproar...

"Out of the heart of earth let man the dead awake,
And let the stars her eyes their pristine spark ignite,
Her golden hair the moon, like it was once, make bright,
While you, o Zamolxis, eternal seed of light,
With breath of fire and frost let her of life partake.

Search wide throughout the kingdom where Harold is
the king

Search deep the very entrails of this revolving earth,
Out of ice make vapour, from stone make gold of worth,
Blood make out of water, and fire from rock give birth,
While in her maiden heart again let hot blood spring."

At that the walls enclosing withdraw before his eyes,
He sees the snow and lightning and ice as one conspire,
The sky, the wind, the water, the elements entire,
He sees a mighty city beneath a bridge of fire,
And over all a thunderstorm of wailing and of sighs.

He sees the Christian church bow 'neath the tempest's host,
He sees the falling lightning its bulwarks shatter through,
The secret tomb within wide open laid to view,
The covering stone of marble divided now in two
And out of that uncovered grave does rise... a ghost.

A thing of snow she is. Upon her bosom frail
A wreath of rubies glows, her hair to earth arrayed,
Her eyes sunk in her head, her lips of violet shade,
Her hands as though of wax upon her temples laid,
Her tender childish face as new slaked lime is pale.

The tumult of her coming does all the clouds dispel,
The lightning and the thunder out of the heavens fly,
The moon turns pitchy-black within a drooping sky,
The waters sink to nowhere and leave the oceans dry;
An angel in her sleep, it seems, who walks through hell.

The vision fades away. Before those gleaming walls,
A form does now approach, with smooth and silent stride;

'Tis she. Harold stares, amazed with joy, wide eyed,
Then reaches out his arms to clasp her to his side,
But in a sudden trance to earth unconscious falls.

He feels two icy hands clasp gently round his heart,
A long and freezing kiss is set upon his breast,
As though from him in sleeping his very life would wrest...
Then feels the life returning to her against him pressed
And knows that from that hour they nevermore will part.

'Tis verily the maid who in her coffin lay?
He feels in her the life yet ever warmer glow,
Till she around his neck her snowy arms does throw,
And raising coaxing lips she says in murmurs low;
"'O King, behold Maria for Harold comes to pray !

Come, Harold, your sweet brow against my bosom lean;
Thou god with eyes of darkness... how wonderful
they shine!
But let me round your neck my golden hair entwine...
My life and youth your presence does in the sky enshrine.
O let me gaze into your eyes of sweet and fatal sheen."

And now a sound of voices does gradually awake,
A song that ancient sweetness upon the ear bestows,
As when a spring at autumn among the dead leaves flows,
A harmony of love, voluptuous repose,
As when in silver cadence the breeze enfolds the lake.

III

"... as often when people die, many of those
dead, they say, wake up to become ghosts..."

In high and empty halls the torches redly burn
Wounding like glowing coals the darkness they intrude;
Harold is striding there in madman's frenzied mood,
Harold, the youthful King; a King in solitude,
While all his palace seems to wait the dead return.

Upon the marble mirrors a heavy shadow rears
Through which the torches' glimmer shines as on silken net,
A twilight doubly mournful with sorrowing beset;
The empty palace chambers house naught but dark regret,
While out of every corner it seems a dead man peers.

Since when the dome was shattered by dreadful light-
ning stroke
The whole day long he passes in cold and leaden sleep,
Upon his heart was branded a symbol black and deep.
But in the night he rises and does his council keep,
And then the pallid king does don his gloomy cloak.

It seems that now a mask of wax King Harold wears,
So paled and so still the face his grief's conceal;
Yet burn his eyes like fires, his lips the blood reveal,
Upon his heart he carries a black and deadly seal,
While on his noble forehead an iron crown he bears.

Since then in death's dark garments he wraps his life forlorn,

He cares but for sad chants as does the tempest play;
Often 'neath the moon at midnight rides away,
And when he does return his eyes are bright and gay
Until death's shuddering voice will grasp him at the dawn.

Harold, what can mean this sombre funeral guise,
This face your wear like wax, so pale and motionless?
What is this seal, this scar that does your heart oppress,
Why do you light the funeral torch, love dirges of distress?
Harold, you are dead if I believe my eyes !

Today once more he mounts his fiery Arab horse
And o'er the wilderness he speeds with arrow's flight
While does the moon shine down her soft and silver light.
Now over the horizon Maria comes in sight,
And through the whispering forest the wind flies on its
course.

Set in her golden hair a wreath of rubies gleams,
The light of many saints does in her large eyes sleep.
On towards the meeting place their chargers swiftly sweep.
They meet and each in greeting bows to the other deep
But on their scarlet lips are stains of blood it seems.

They gallop like the tempest with thousand wings, they fly
Speeding o'er the country their chargers side by side,
Speaking of their love that naught can more divide,
She rests upon his arm that is around her plied
And on his ready shoulder her golden head does lie.

"Come Harold, your sweet brow upon my bosom lean

Thou God with eyes of darkness... how beautiful they
shine !
But let me round your neck my golden hair entwine...
My life and youth your presence does in the sky enshrine.
O let me gaze into your eyes of sweet and fatal sheen."

A soft and soothing scent is in the air dispersed,
A shower of lime-tree blossoms the wind in passing throws
Upon the way by which the Queen of Danube goes,
A murmuring of breezes among the petals blows,
While do in tender kiss unite their lips athirst.

Thus flying like the wind they each of love inquire,
Nor see beyond the night the dawn already glowing;
Yet in their souls they feel an icy shiver growing
And o'er their pallid faces a mask of death is showing
While slowly on their lips their whispered words expire.

"O Harold, on your breast allow my face to hide,
Do you not hear far off the cock's hoarse morning cry?
A spear of light that sprang athwart the eastern sky
To wound his fleeting life within my heart does pry;
Within my soul is born the ruddy fire of day."

Harold bolt upright was stricken like an oak,
His eyes forever veiled with death's eternal shade.
Their steeds fled on untended with panic dread afraid,
Like to a demon's shadow straight out of Hades strayed
They went... Among the trees a plaintive wind awoke.

They speed on like a whirlwind, cross rivers no bridge
spanned.
Before their flying course the dawn-lit mountains gleam,
They traverse hill and valley, and many a fordless stream,
Upon their waxen foreheads their crowns like light-
ning beam,
While far away before them the pine-tree forests stand.

Now from his rocky throne the old magician spies
Their coming, and he calls above the tempest fray
The sun to check its course, the night its moon delay,
The gale to fly abroad, the earth its movement stay,
Too late... The rising sun is mounting up the skies.

The hurricane let loose a tale of pain relates
And sweeps along besides them to fill their steeds
with dread;
Their eyes are dimmed and downcast, the fire in them
is shed,
Beautiful their dying, in death forever wed.
Now, widely swinging, open the temple's double gates.

They ride into the temple, the gates behind them swing.
Lost for all eternity within the tomb's constraint;
Around them in the darkness there sounds a sad complaint
For that fair mortal maid whose face was of a saint,
For Harold, youthful monarch, the pine-tree forest's king.

The Seer now lowers his eyebrows, the world fades from
His feet into the granite again enrooted grow,
Numbering the days that numberless did flow,

Harold in his failing mind a tale of long ago,
While soaring o'er his head two crows: one black, one white.

Upon his rocky ledge, upright and ashen faced,
There sits with crutch in hand the priest of pagan creed.
For ages sits he thus, by death forgot indeed,
Moss growing on his forehead and on his breast long weed,
His beard reaching to the ground, his eyebrows to his waist.

(Translated by Corneliu M. Popescu)

Strigoii

George Bacovia

VAMPIRES IN LITERATURE

With red lanterns, yellow, green
The vampires pass in night over wheat
And the dogs bark on in the night at the fields
The vampires have entered the loft of an inn,
And the loft is seen to be queerly lit
By red lanterns, yellow, green.

The vampires have returned to the loft to retrieve
Pledges left long ago in their lives ...
So goes a story that now I've forgotten
That at night, in the inn, there appear silhouettes
With red lanterns, yellow, green.

But when the cock crows toward daybreak,
In a pack the vampires tumbles out of the loft,
`Cross the fields, and in chaos they all disappear,
Either red, yellow or green.

Croglin Grange
Alan Frost

VAMPIRES IN LITERATURE

A curious place was old Croglin Grange,
with a graveyard and church in plain view.
And a girl sleeps in fear, one night in some year
of which I admit there's no clue.
From the trees outside, there appears a face,
two flickering lights do fix her gaze.
Nearer now, larger, something
ghastly emerges: eyes ablaze
it approaches, on and on,
til it clings to her windowpane,
this fiendish, unearthly one.
Scratch. Scratch. Scratch.
It finds the latch, and creeps inside,
bony fingers primed for violence.
Embracing her neck,
a smile; a gloat.
She cries out, but only silence
now quenches her throat.

The Poet Talks with the Biographers
Clark Ashton Smith

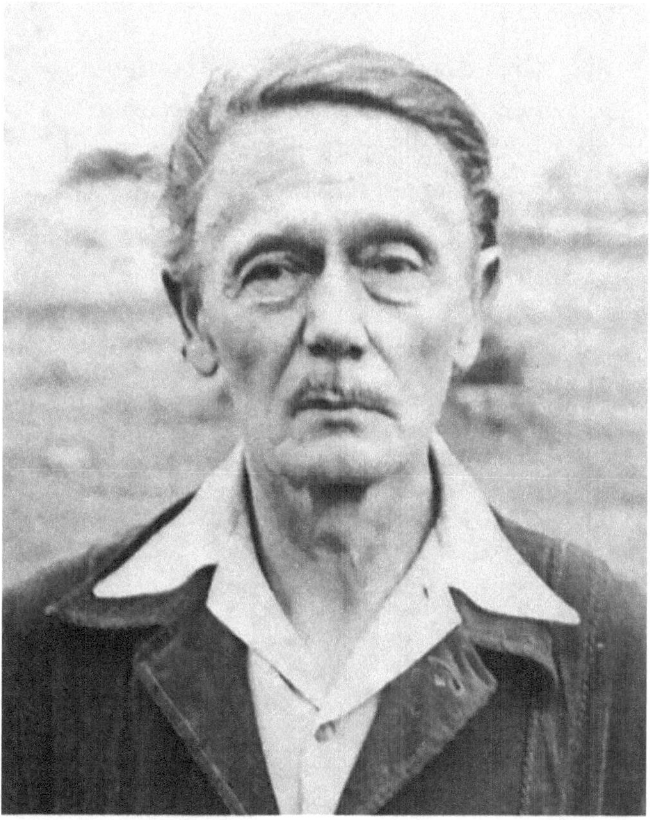

O ghouls of fetid and funereal midnights,
Say, what do you uncover in your sad labors?
—We have disinterred the Empusa of thy fears
And the frightful Gorgon with her livid eyeballs
In our mournful labors.

O diggers all so diligent, O sapient ghouls,
What have you found in your prodigious toils?
—We have exhumed with all their antique evils
Thy loves, with features gutted by the worms,
In our enormous toils.

Grimed openers of pyramid and ossuary,
What revealed ye yesterday at crimson evening?
—We have dug up the black and ashen soil
To anatomize the shroudless nymph
Who was laid to sleep at evening.

Ghouls, what would ye do, tonight, for your pleasure,
Within these low, lugubrious and gaping tombs?
—We come to disenswathe the living dead—
The never-gelded fauns of thine old vices—
Within these gaping tombs.

Notes

Excerpt from Voltaire's Philosophical Dictionary; (Translation by William F. Fleming, 1901):

What! is it in our eighteenth century that vampires exist? Is it after the reigns of Locke, Shaftesbury, Trenchard, and Collins? Is it under those of d'Alembert, Diderot, St. Lambert, and Duclos that we believe in vampires, and that the reverend father Dom Calmet, Benedictine priest of the congregation of St. Vannes, and St. Hidulphe, abbé of Senon—an abbey of a hundred thousand livres a year, in the neighborhood of two other abbeys of the same revenue—has printed and reprinted the history of vampires, with the approbation of the Sorbonne, signed Marcilli?

These vampires were corpses, who went out of their graves at night to suck the blood of the living, either at their throats or stomachs, after which they returned to their cemeteries. The persons so sucked waned, grew pale, and fell into consumption; while the sucking corpses grew fat, got rosy, and enjoyed an excellent appetite. It was in Poland, Hungary, Silesia, Moravia, Austria, and Lorraine, that the dead made this good cheer. We never heard a word of vampires in London, nor even at Paris. I confess that in both these cities there were stock-jobbers, brokers, and men of business, who sucked the blood of the people in broad daylight; but they were not dead, though corrupted. These true suckers lived not in cemeteries, but in very agreeable palaces.

Who would believe that we derive the idea of vampires from Greece? Not from the Greece of Alexander, Aristotle, Plato, Epicurus, and Demosthenes; but from Christian Greece, unfortunately schismatic. For a long time Christians of the Greek rite have imagined that the bodies of Christians of the Latin church, buried in Greece, do not decay, because they are excommunicated. This is precisely the contrary to that of us Christians of the Latin church, who believe that corpses which do not corrupt are marked with the seal of eternal beatitude. So much so, indeed, that when we have paid a hundred thousand crowns to Rome, to give them a saint's brevet, we adore them with the worship of "dulia."

The Greeks are persuaded that these dead are sorcerers; they call them "broucolacas," or "vroucolacas," according as they pronounce the second letter of the alphabet. The Greek corpses go into houses to suck the blood of little children, to eat the supper of the fathers and mothers, drink their wine, and break all the furniture. They can only be put to rights by burning them when they are caught. But the precaution must be taken of not putting them into the fire until after their hearts are torn out, which must be burned separately. The celebrated Tournefort, sent into the Levant by Louis XIV., as well as so many other virtuosi, was witness of all the acts attributed to one of these "broucolacas," and to this ceremony.

After slander, nothing is communicated more promptly than superstition, fanaticism, sorcery, and tales of those raised from the dead. There were "broucolacas" in Wallachia, Moldavia, and some among the Polanders, who are of the Romish church. This superstition being absent, they acquired it, and it went through all the east of Germany. Nothing was spoken of but vampires, from 1730 to 1735; they were laid in wait for, their hearts torn out and burned. They resembled the ancient martyrs—the more they were burned, the more they abounded.

Finally, Calmet became their historian, and treated vampires as he treated the Old and New Testaments, by relating faithfully all that has been said before him.

The most curious things, in my opinion, were the verbal suits juridically conducted, concerning the dead who went from their tombs to suck the little boys and girls of their neighborhood. Calmet relates that in Hungary two officers, delegated by the emperor Charles VI., assisted by the bailiff of the place and an executioner, held an inquest on a vampire, who had been dead six weeks, and who had sucked all the neighborhood. They found him in his coffin, fresh and jolly, with his eyes open, and asking for food. The bailiff passed his sentence; the executioner tore out the vampire's heart, and burned it, after which he feasted no more.

Who, after this, dares to doubt of the resuscitated dead, with which our ancient legends are filled, and of all the miracles related by Bollandus, and the sincere and revered Dom Ruinart? You will find stories of vampires in the "Jewish Letters" of d'Argens, whom the Jesuit authors of the "Journal of Trévoux" have accused of believing nothing. It should be observed how they triumph in the history of the vampire of Hungary; how they thanked God and the Virgin for having at last converted this poor d'Argens, the chamberlain of a king who did not believe in vampires. "Behold," said they, "this famous unbeliever, who dared to throw doubts on the appearance of the angel to the Holy Virgin; on the star which conducted the magi; on the cure of the possessed; on the immersion of two thousand swine in a lake; on an eclipse of the sun at the full moon; on the resurrection of the dead who walked in Jerusalem—his heart is softened, his mind is enlightened; he believes in vampires."

There no longer remained any question, but to examine whether all these dead were raised by their own virtue, by the power of God, or by that of the devil. Several great theologians of Lorraine, of Moravia, and Hungary, displayed their opinions and their science. They related all that St. Augustine, St. Ambrose, and so many other saints, had most unintelligibly said on the living and the dead. They related all the miracles of St. Stephen, which are found in the seventh book of the works of St. Augustine. This is one of the most curious of them: In the city of Aubzal in Africa, a young man was crushed to death by the ruins of a wall; the widow immediately invoked St. Stephen, to whom she was very much devoted. St. Stephen raised him. He was asked what he had seen in the other world. "Sirs," said he, "when my soul quitted my body, it met an infinity of souls, who asked it more questions about this world than you do of the other. I went I know not whither, when I met St. Stephen, who said to me, 'Give back that which thou hast received.' I answered, 'What should I give back? you have given me nothing.' He repeated three times, 'Give back that which thou hast received.' Then I comprehended that he spoke of the credo; I repeated my credo to him, and suddenly he raised me." Above all, they quoted the stories related by Sulpicius Severus, in the life of St. Martin. They proved that St. Martin, with some others, raised up a condemned soul.

But all these stories, however true they might be, had nothing in common with the vampires who rose to suck the blood of their neighbors, and afterwards replaced themselves in their coffins. They looked if they could not find in the Old Testament, or in the mythology, some vampire whom they could quote as an example; but they found none. It was proved, however, that the dead drank and ate, since in so many ancient nations food was placed on their tombs.

The difficulty was to know whether it was the soul or the body of the dead which ate. It was decided that it was both. Delicate and unsubstantial things, as sweetmeats, whipped cream, and melting fruits, were for the soul, and roast beef and the like were for the body.

The kings of Persia were, said they, the first who caused themselves to be served with viands after their death. Almost all the kings of the present day imitate them; but they are the monks who eat their dinner and supper, and drink their wine. Thus, properly speaking, kings are not vampires; the true vampires are the monks, who eat at the expense of both kings and people.

It is very true that St. Stanislaus, who had bought a considerable estate from a Polish gentleman, and not paid him for it, being brought before King Boleslaus by his heirs, raised up the gentleman; but this was solely to get quittance. It is not said that he gave a single glass of wine to the seller, who returned to the other world without having eaten or drunk. They afterwards treated of the grand question, whether a vampire could be absolved who died excommunicated, which comes more to the point.

I am not profound enough in theology to give my opinion on this subject; but I would willingly be for absolution, because in all doubtful affairs we should take the mildest part. "Odia restringenda, favores ampliandi."

The result of all this is that a great part of Europe has been infested with vampires for five or six years, and that there are now no more; that we have had Convulsionaries in France for twenty years, and that we have them no longer; that we have had demoniacs for seventeen hundred years, but have them no longer; that the dead have been raised ever since the days of Hippolytus, but that they are raised no longer; and, lastly, that we have had Jesuits in Spain, Portugal, France, and the two Sicilies, but that we have them no longer.

Berwick-Upon-Tweed

The northerly town in England known as Berwick-Upon Tweed has had several ghost and/or vampire events. Many of these accounts are considered more reliable because they were chronicled by the respected William of Newburgh (William Parvus).

One of the more popular documented accounts:

"Among the incidents of vampirism reported by William of Newburgh in his Chronicles, completed in 1196 C.E., was the case of the Berwick vampire. The subject of the account was a rather wealthy man who lived in the twelfth century in the town of Berwick in the northern part of England near the Scottish border. After his death, the townspeople reported seeing his body roaming through the streets at night keeping the dogs howling far into the evening. Fearful that a plague (associated with such revenants in popular lore) might attack the population, the townspeople decided to dismember the body and burn it. That action having been accomplished, the body no longer appeared in town; however, a disease did sweep through the town causing many deaths that were attributed to the after-effects of the vampire's presence."

"Berwick, The Vampire of." The Vampire Book, Second Edition. 2011. Visible Ink Press 31 Oct. 2024
https://encyclopedia2.thefreedictionary.com/Berwick%2c+The+Vampire+of

Bride of Corinth Based On

"The Bride of Corinth" was based on a Greek story, "Philinnion and Machates" written in second-century A.D. by Phlegon of Tralles. Many consider this Greek story to be the first "Vampire Romance". Although Phlegon did not directly state it, there is a strong implication in the original story (and language) that Philinnion did drink Machates blood while he slept.

Below is a translation of this Greek story. The first few sentences are lost. We begin at the point in which Philinnion has been dead for many months, but she has been visiting the young man who has been sleeping in her room. His name is Machates, One night, a nurse walks in and sees the two sitting on the bed together.

The nurse went to the door of the guest room, and in the light of the burning lamp she saw the girl sitting beside Machates. Because of the extraordinary nature of the sight, she did not wait there any longer but ran to the girl's mother screaming, `Kharito! Demostratos!' She *said they should get up and come with her to their daughter, who was alive and by some divine will was with the guest in the guest room.*

When Kharito heard this astonishing report, the immensity of the message and the nurse's excitement made her frightened and faint. But after a short time the memory of her daughter came to her, and she began to weep; in the end she accused the old woman of being mad and told her to leave her presence immediately. But the nurse replied boldly and reproachfully that she herself was rational and sound of mind, unlike her mistress, who was reluctant to see her own daughter. With some hesitation Kharito went to the door of the guest room, partly coerced by the nurse and partly wanting to know what really had happened. Since considerable time—about two hours— had now passed since the nurse's original message, it was somewhat late when Kharito went to the door and the occupants were already asleep. She peered in and, though she recognized her daughter's clothes and features, but inasmuch as she could not determine the truth of the matter, she decided to do nothing further that night. She planned to get up in the morning and confront the girl, or if she should be too late for that, she intended to question Machates thoroughly about everything. He would not, she thought, lie if asked about so important a matter. And so she said nothing and left.

At dawn, however, it turned out that by divine will or chance the girl had left unnoticed. When Kharito came to the room she was upset with the young man because of the girl's departure. She asked him to relate everything to her from the beginning, telling the truth and concealing nothing.

The youth was anxious and confused at first, but hesitantly revealed the girl's name was Philinnion. He told how her visits began, how great her desire for him was, and that she said she came to him without her parents' knowledge. Wishing to make the matter credible he opened his coffer and took out the items the girl had left behind - the golden ring he had obtained from her and the breast-band she had left the night before.

When Kharito saw this evidence she uttered a cry, tore her clothes, cast her headdress from her head and fell to the ground, throwing herself upon the tokens and beginning her grief anew. As the guest observed what was happening, how all were grieving and wailing as if they were about to lay the girl into her grave, he became upset and called upon them to stop, promising to show them the girl if she came again. Kharito accepted this and bade him carefully keep his promise to her.

Night came on and now it was the hour when Philinnion was accustomed to come to him. The household kept watch wanting to know of her arrival. She entered at the usual time and sat down on the bed. Machates pretended that nothing was wrong, since he wished to investigate the whole incredible matter to find out if the girl he was consorting with, who took care to come to him at the same hour, was actually dead. As she ate and drank with him, he simply could not believe what the others had told him, and he supposed that some grave-robbers had dug into the tomb and sold the clothes and gold to her father. But in his wish to learn exactly what the case was, he secretly sent his slaves to summon Demostratos and Kharito.

They came quickly. When they first saw her they were speechless and panic-stricken by the amazing sight, but after that they cried aloud and embraced their daughter. Then Philinnion said to them : `Mother and father, how unfairly you have grudged my being with the guest for three days in my father's house, since I have caused no one any pain. For this reason, on account of your meddling, you shall grieve all over again, and I shall return to the place appointed for me. For it was not without divine will that I came here.' Immediately upon speaking these words she was dead, and her body lay stretched visibly on the bed. Her father and mother threw themselves upon her, and there was much confusion and wailing in the house because of the calamity. The misfortune was unbearable and the sight incredible.

The event was quickly heard through the city and was reported to me. Accordingly, during the night I kept in check the crowds that gathered at the house, since, with news like this going from mouth to mouth, I wanted to make sure there would be no trouble.

By early dawn the town assembly was full. After the particulars had been explained, it was decided that we should first go to the tomb, open it, and see whether the body lay on its bier or whether we would find the place empty. A half-year had not yet passed since the death of the girl. When we opened the chamber into which all deceased members of the family were placed, we saw bodies lying on biers, or bones in the case of those who had died long ago, but on the bier onto which Philinnion had been placed we found only the iron ring that belonged to the guest and the gilded wine cup, objects that she had obtained from Machates on the first day.

Astonished and frightened, we proceeded immediately to Demostratos's house to see if the corpse was truly to be seen in the guest room. After we saw the dead girl lying there on the ground, we gathered at the place of assembly, since the events were serious and incredible.

There was considerable confusion in the assembly and almost no one was able to form a judgment on the events. The first to stand up was Hyllos, who is considered to be not only the best seer among us but also a fine augur; in general, he has shown remarkable perception in his craft. He said we should burn the girl outside the boundaries of the city, since nothing would be gained by burying her in the ground within its boundaries, and perform an apotropaic sacrifice to Hermes, Khthonios and the Eumenides. Then he prescribed that everyone purify himself completely, cleanse the temples and perform all the customary rites to the Khthonion [underworld] gods. He spoke to me also in private about the king and the events, telling me to sacrifice to Hermes, Zeus, Xenios, and Ares, and to perform these rites with care. When he had made this known to us, we undertook to do what he had prescribed. Machates, the guest whom the ghost had visited, became despondent and killed himself.

If you decide to write about this to the king, send word to me also in order that I may dispatch to you one of the persons who examined the affair in detail. Farewell.

We hope you enjoyed this foreword volume to the Vampires in Literature Collection.

Be sure to see future volumes.

Next: